I0777742

Blame It On The Reindeer

Samantha Baca

<u>Sugarplum Falls Series</u>

Blame It On The Mistletoe

Blame It On The Eggnog

Blame It On The Candy Canes

Blame It On The Blizzard

Blame It On The Reindeer

Blame It On The Carols

Blame It On The Lattes

Blame It On The Secret Santa

Copyright © 2024 by Samantha Baca.

All rights reserved. If you are reading this book and did not purchase it, this book has been pirated, and you are stealing. Please delete it from your device and support the author by purchasing a legal copy.
All rights reserved. No part of this book may be reproduced or transmitted in any form or by any means, electronic or mechanical, including photocopying, recording, or by information storage and retrieval system, without written permission of the publisher, except where permitted by law. This book is a work of fiction. Names, places, characters, and incidents are the product of the author's imagination or are used fictitiously.

Cover Design: Richard Baca
Image (s): DepositPhotos

Contents

<u>One</u>
Jasmin

"What do you mean *he's dead*?" I asked, leaning forward to hang onto every word out of Sam's mouth as I sipped my gingerbread latte.

"He died." He shrugged, smiling and waving at the customer who was leaving. "I heard about it this morning. He passed about a week ago, but the family has been busy dealing with stuff, so they haven't been in town much until today."

"He can't be dead." I shook my head in disbelief as Sugarplum Lattes got in the full swing of their morning rush. There was a reason it was the busiest coffee shop in Sugarplum Falls, and it wasn't just because the barista was incredibly handsome with dimples that could kill. No, people from neighboring towns came flocking to it for the incredible holiday-inspired drinks that Sam created this time of year, forcing the locals to come in early just to get their fix.

"Well, I hate to break it to you, but I'm pretty sure he is. Went in his sleep."

Sam wiped down the counter and nodded at Andi, the owner of Sugarplum Sweets, before returning his attention to me.

"This is literally the *worst* timing ever," I mumbled, my coffee suddenly tasting bitter despite the extra syrup I'd requested. "How could he do this to me?"

"Well, technically, I don't think he *meant* to do it, nor was it directed at you. I mean, he was ninety years old, Jas. It was kind of bound to happen." He leaned against the counter, crossing one ankle over the other while he kept an eye on the new employee running the register. I knew I only had a few minutes to chat with him before he'd have to take over with the line that was going to form.

"Yeah, but still—*two weeks* before Frosty Fest? That's just downright mean. He could have at least tried to get through one more before he just quit. Doesn't he know the bind he's putting us in?"

"Again," he said lightly with a laugh. "I don't think he did this to you on purpose. He was old, and his health was getting worse. You remember how bad it was last year when it took him over three hours to make it the thirty minutes into town from his farm? His body was tired, Jas."

"I know." I exhaled heavily, feeling like a total jerk. "I'm sorry, I'm just stressed with things already going sideways with Frosty Fest, and this just takes the cake. How am I supposed to do this without any reindeer?"

"I heard his grandson is moving back to take over the farm," Andi said, reaching past me to grab a straw from the counter. Sugarplum Sweets was a few shops over in the strip mall, so it didn't surprise me that she was already getting filled in on the gossip this morning as well since most locals grabbed their coffee from Sam and then headed over for a pastry from Andi. "Maybe you could ask him to help out?"

"I think she has a better chance of meeting a knight in shining armor than getting Brody to help out," Sam replied with a cheeky smile.

"What's that supposed to mean?" I narrowed my eyes, glaring at him.

"It means he's a crotchety guy, and from what I've heard, he's not *our type*."

My eyebrows shot up as I gave Andi a questioning glance. She shrugged, equally confused. Apparently, she hadn't heard *all* of the gossip yet.

"Like he's into other men? Because I have no problem with that. Some of my best friends—"

"No," Sam interrupted, holding his hand up to stop me. "He's not the *Christmas* type."

My jaw dropped open as I processed that disturbing bit of news. There were a lot of things in life I could handle disagreements over, but not liking Christmas wasn't one of them.

"What? How is that possible?"

"I don't know, but apparently, he's not big on the holiday. From what his mom said, he's more of the grinch type."

"You can't live in Sugarplum Falls and *not* like Christmas. That's like blasphemy." A shiver ran over my body as I thought about it. How could anyone not like Christmas? It was the best time of the year.

"Yet that's exactly what I'm saying. It's never been his thing, according to her."

Sam tended to get the town's gossip quicker than anyone—likely because he was so personable that he was easy to talk to, and everyone in a small town loved to talk about other people. But for me, this was proving to be beneficial because now I could try to get ahead of things before they got too far out of control. I didn't want this year to be the year that I failed with Frosty Fest, but there were plenty of things already stacking against me. While it might be challenging to convince someone who hated Christmas to do something super Christmassy, I wasn't going to give up that easily. I was born a fighter, and I wouldn't go down without a fight. One way or another, I would have those reindeer.

"That's it!" I exclaimed excitedly, a surge of clarity washing over me. "I'll just talk to his mom. Surely, she'll understand the importance of having the reindeer at Frosty Fest and will get him to help us. It doesn't matter if he doesn't like the holiday as long as we get the reindeer. She can help orchestrate everything since Mr. Truman is gone, then Brody won't have to be involved other than delivering the animals. It's a win-win for everyone."

"I love your enthusiasm," Sam said lightly, his eyes softening with pity. "But I don't think that's going to work. He hasn't spoken to her in over fifteen years. Apparently, they had a big falling out, and he moved to Wyoming, never bothering to look back. He hasn't had contact with most of his family since then."

"Of course he hasn't." I shook my head, trying to keep up. This was a lot to take in this early on a Monday morning, but it was essential to have all of the details so I could figure out my next step. If I could fully understand what the problem was, I could fix it. "So why is he back now? If he walked away from his family and didn't want anything to do with them, why come back?"

I felt like I was getting whiplash from all of the back and forth, but then again, that could also be from the extra shot of espresso I ordered in my drink this morning. What he was saying made sense, but yet it didn't. Why come back to a place you purposely left, especially if you have no interest in reuniting with your family?

"From what I heard, his grandfather left him the ranch. He was the only one that Brody kept in contact with, but no one knew about it until recently when Mr. Truman started to get ill. He told them that he had left the ranch to Brody and that no one should contest it. That was his final request."

"So what you're saying is that I'm stuck dealing with a cranky, non-Christmas loving, grumpy ass man from out of town?" I raised my eyebrows, hoping he would correct me.

"It kinda looks like it."

I leaned back and allowed my shoulders to slump as I accepted reality.

"What are you going to do?" Andi asked, taking a sip of her iced coffee.

"The only thing I can."

I took a deep breath in and slowly let it out as I tried to force my body to relax. This wasn't the kind of news I had hoped for today, but there was no other way around it. It sucked that I would have a harder time securing the reindeer for Frosty Fest, but I couldn't let the town down by not trying. They were counting on me to bring in the traffic that would drive their holiday sales through the roof and give them the financial security they needed. I had watched my parents struggle to make ends meet while I was growing up, especially around the holidays. I knew how much of an impact this event had on our community and I couldn't swallow the bitter pill of failing this year. No matter what it took, I had to try.

"I'm going to convince him to help me. To help Sugarplum Falls. We need Frosty Fest to drive business from nearby towns, so I'm going to make sure it goes off without a hitch. The town is counting on me, and I refuse to let them down. Frosty Fest *has* to happen—there's no other option." I grabbed my purse and coffee cup from the counter.

"Good luck. Keep us posted," Sam called as I headed for the door.

I smiled over my shoulder, pretending to be more confident than I felt.

Two
Brody

"Go away," I replied to the incessant knocking on the front door.

I hadn't been in Sugarplum Falls long, but I had hoped that I would be able to go a few more weeks before the town showed up, wanting to introduce themselves and offer their condolences about my grandfather.

When I got the phone call from him a few months ago that things were declining with his health, I started making arrangements to get out here. I didn't expect him to pass the day before I showed up, not getting to say my final goodbye to him.

"Hi, I'm looking for Brody," a female voice called loudly through the door.

It wasn't like I knew anyone in town since I moved fifteen years ago at the ripe age of eighteen, and I wanted to keep it that way. My grandfather's ranch was a good thirty minutes outside of Sugarplum Falls, which was the closest town. This worked well for him since he always preferred to live in the middle of nowhere. People used to say he was crazy to want to live such a solitary life, but I understood it. It was calm and peaceful without people constantly being in your business.

"I'm not interested," I growled back, picking up the stack of papers I still needed to go through from the stuff my grandfather's lawyer had given me.

"It would be a lot easier to have this conversation if you would just open the door and talk to me," she replied, sounding impatient. "I'm not trying to take up more time here than I have to, but I really need to talk to you."

I rolled my head back on my neck, trying to alleviate some of the mounting tension.

"Is this about my extended car warranty?" I asked, pulling the door open enough to see the petite brunette on the other side without giving the impression of a warm invite. "Or are you here to sell cookies?"

The curves of her body and her plump, round breasts screamed that she was old enough to sell more than cookies—and whatever she was selling was something I would be interested in buying. Full lips pursed as golden flecks of amber sparkled in the brown eyes that were now narrowed at me.

"No." Her thin, perfectly groomed brows furrowed deeper. "I'm here because I run the Frosty Fest—"

"Frosty Fest?" I questioned, interrupting her with a raised eyebrow. "Please tell me that isn't some ridiculous festival of snowmen."

She cocked her head to the side and glared at me.

"No, it's not a ridic—" She stopped and snapped her mouth shut, eyes fluttering wildly as if she was trying to regain her composure. "The reason I'm here is because I run the festival, and every year, Mr. Trum—*your grandfather,* would assist us with bringing the reindeer down for the parade. Since he's passed—sorry for your loss, by the way—I was hoping that I could make arrangements with you for this year's festival. I know you have a lot on your plate right now with taking care of his estate, but if you can let me know when is a good time to send someone to collect the reindeer, I can—"

"Sorry, that's not going to happen. Thank you for stopping by."

I started to close the door when a skinny leather boot with a pointy heel stepped forward and stopped it.

"Look, I know you might not want to talk about this right now, and I get that you're busy," she objected, tucking a strand of dark brown wavy hair behind her ear. "I'm busy too. Running Frosty Fest is my job, and I can't do my job without the reindeer."

"Sounds like a you problem." I folded my arms over my chest, not budging.

Typically I would have already slammed the door shut and not given a damn about who or what was on the other side, but with her, I found myself stalling to shut her out. Maybe it was because I hadn't seen a woman as beautiful as her in a long time, or perhaps it was because her fiery little attitude stirred something deep inside of me and I liked it.

"It is, but it doesn't have to be if you would just look in that icy cold heart of yours and do the right thing."

I arched an eyebrow, wondering how all that sass could come out of something so small. I was intrigued, to say the least, but now wasn't the time to entertain this. I had stuff to get done, and she was wasting my time on this nonsense.

"I hate to break it to you, but nothing will ever thaw my ice-cold heart. It's probably better that you accept that now. Thanks for stopping by, but my answer is no."

I watched her chest rise and fall heavily as she stared at me with defeat before I closed the door. I didn't want to be a dick, but I wasn't here to make friends. The less I got involved with the people of Sugarplum Falls, the better off I would be.

Three
Jasmin

"How did it go?" Andi asked as I sat at the end of the counter and stuffed another truffle in my mouth.

"It's ten o'clock in the morning, and I've eaten all of the samples you guys have out. How do you think it went?" I replied around a mouthful of delicious chocolate and coconut. "These are amazing, by the way. Tell Zach he really outdid himself."

"I'll let him know when he's done making the current batch." She stacked boxes of pre-packaged chocolates on the table by the register, arranging them accordingly before stepping back and looking at them.

"It looks great. I think those will sell fast," I commented, already eyeing which ones would be going home with me. Not that I needed more chocolate given the amount I'd already consumed this morning, but it was the holiday season and nothing said *happy holidays* like a stockpile of sweets.

"Thanks. We sold out of the fudge and dark chocolate truffles yesterday, so I'm trying to anticipate what our bestsellers are going to be for Frosty Fest. Last year, we sold out midday. I don't want that to happen again."

"Well, let's see if we even have a Frosty Fest this year," I replied sarcastically around another bite.

"We will," she assured me. "Even if we don't have the reindeer, we can still make the festival happen."

"How?" I crumpled up the napkin I had been using and tossed it in the trash. "People come from neighboring towns because we have reindeer and Santa and Mrs. Claus—which, by the way—I'm about to fire a few elves. But that's a whole other story. My point is that people come *here* because they want that Christmas feeling. They bring their kids because our Santa looks so much like the real thing, it adds that magic into the holidays for them. If we don't have the reindeer for the kids to feed, then they don't have a reason to come see us. You can't have Christmas in Sugarplum Falls without the reindeer."

"I know. But maybe we just have to embrace the change and move forward."

She smiled softly at me, but it did nothing to lessen the vise grip that was squeezing my heart at the thought of the local town kids who would be disappointed this year as well. It wasn't just the out-of-town business that we needed for our event to thrive; it was the happiness that you could feel when walking Main Street or visiting with the locals while being encompassed in holiday bliss.

"I have the next batch ready," Zach said as he came through the doors that led to the kitchen. He stopped short when he saw me, a panicked look on his face.

"Don't worry, I won't touch those." I held my hands in front of me and smiled. "I'm going to grab a few things and then get out of here. I need to go find my zen so I can clear my mind and get back to planning."

"Well, if you need any help, you know where to go," Andi

replied softly, taking the tray of truffles from Zach and lining them up on the sample plate by the register.

"Sugar Faced Bar?" I teased.

She placed her hands on her hips and tilted her head as she pinned me with a look.

"What? Aiden makes a killer dirty snowman."

"I don't even want to know." Andi shook her head but I noticed the corners of her lips tilting up into a smile.

"Trust me, it's just a drink. If you don't like that, he also makes a fantastic mistletoe margarita. Ooh, or a gingerbread martini!"

"I think you're spending way too much time at the bar," she teased.

"Or perhaps you're not spending enough time there. I'm just saying I see Sam in the morning for my holiday latte to start my day and Aiden when I'm wrapping up for the day and need a holiday cocktail to wind down. Between both of them, I have everything I could need in life." I smiled and shrugged my shoulders.

"Except for reindeer," Zach said with a cheeky smile, ducking as Andi tossed the towel he brought out at his head. "What? It's true."

"And see, this depressing news is why I'm heading over to see Aiden." I sighed heavily as I grabbed my stuff—along with three boxes of chocolates I needed to buy.

"It's not even noon," Andi objected, her head shaking as she rang me up.

"No. But it's five o'clock somewhere."

Four
Brody

I stood at the fence, examining the damage to the posts that needed to be fixed. My grandfather had mentioned that he needed to redo it, he just hadn't gotten around to it before he got sick. After that, his body never recovered to what it was before, which left him unable to do a lot of the stuff he needed to.

I pulled my phone out of my pocket and added a quick note of what I needed to grab at the hardware store. For now, the reindeer were secure in their pen, but one good gust of wind would be all it took to dismantle everything. And according to the news this morning, we were expecting to get a nasty storm rolling in this week.

The temperature outside had already dropped dramatically, reminding me of Christmases spent at the ranch with my grandfather growing up. It was bittersweet to be back here without him. The pain of losing him was more than I expected, but the regrets of not coming back sooner and spending his last days with him were what really ate at me.

I couldn't undo the past, but I could honor him by taking care of what he left to me. The ranch was his pride and joy, and I took comfort in knowing that he trusted me to continue his legacy. Even if I felt like I had no idea what his intentions were with letting that crazy woman use the reindeer for some snowman festival.

After checking the gate, I secured the latch on it and gave it a quick shake to make sure it wouldn't open while I was gone. The last thing I needed was to come back to the reindeer making a run for it. I wasn't planning to be gone long, but I learned early on that if you were making a stop in town, you got everything while you were there to save you from having to go back. It was only a thirty-minute drive into town, which wasn't bad. It was having to talk to people that made my skin crawl.

****

By the time I got back from running errands in town my jaw was locked from how tightly I clenched it as I tried to power through everyone wanting to talk to me. Most of them simply offered their condolences and moved on, but a handful of them wanted to talk my ear off and didn't get the message that I wasn't interested in talking as I ignored them.

I was relieved to hit the dirt road that led to the ranch, even if it was covered in a blanket of snow. I had hoped to get back before the storm started, but things in a small town tended to move painfully slowly. Thankfully, the drive was beautiful nonetheless, with snow-covered trees that lined the side of the road.

As I rounded the corner to the ranch, I slowed down, leaning forward to get a glimpse of the SUV parked in front of the house. I wasn't expecting company, which made my frustration rise to the surface again.

I put the truck in park and got out, looking around to see who was there. The Tahoe was empty, which meant someone was stupid enough to be out trespassing on private property, likely putting their nose where it didn't belong. I grabbed the bags from the front seat and slammed the door, knowing the sound of the old metal truck would be loud enough for whoever was out there to hear.

By the time I got everything unpacked from the truck, I had yet to see who was still parked on my property. I didn't expect there to be any trouble, given that the ranch was in the middle of nowhere and was pretty hard to find unless you knew it was there. Still, it made me uneasy knowing that someone had obviously found it and was making themselves at home without my permission.

I started a pot of coffee so it would be ready when I got back—Lord knew I would need the energy today. Then I grabbed my keys from the counter, stuffed them in my pocket, and closed the door behind me as I went in search of the intruder.

Five
Jasmin

"You have got to be kidding me," I grumbled, wiggling as I tried to free myself from my jacket that was now stuck around a fence post. How it happened—I had not a fucking clue.

I grabbed the zipper and tried yanking it down again, knowing that if I could get it unzipped, I could easily be free. The last thing I wanted was to get caught out here, stuck to the crabby ass guy's fence like some moron. Though, I guess it was only fair to say that I shouldn't have been snooping around if I didn't want to risk getting caught.

My body was starting to go cold from the frigid temperatures outside as worry nagged at my brain about the risk of possibly losing a limb to frostbite. I had no idea how long I had been stuck because every second that passed felt like hours. For all I knew, it could have been months and Frosty Fest was now a thing of the past.

I wiggled my fingers, hoping to get some feeling back into them as I attempted to work the zipper down once again. My feet ached from the wetness that had seeped into the fabric of my boots from the snow on the ground, as well as from awkwardly standing in one spot for so long. Who knew that having a wooden post attached to your back would make it impossible to move your body?

"Would you care to explain this?" a gruff voice said from behind me, the sound of footsteps crunching in the snow.

Shit.

"It's actually a funny story," I lied, knowing my face was beet red from embarrassment as well as the cold.

He arched an eyebrow as he stood in front of me, his dirty blonde hair covered by a thick beanie pulled down over his head. I had been entranced by his hazel eyes when I saw him yesterday, but today they were mesmerizing as they sparkled against the snow falling behind him.

"I came to bring you something," I continued, hating how stupid I must look pinned to the post as he made no effort to try to help me.

His arms folded over his chest, the thick winter coat he was wearing doing nothing to hide the muscular body beneath it.

"A cookie. Well, cookie*s*. I brought more than one." I shook my head, irritated by my own rambling. "I thought you might want to eat my cookie while we talked."

A ghost of a smile fluttered across his face before it disappeared, sending a jolt straight through me.

"I don't mean *eat my cookie*—that's gross. I mean, eat a cookie that I brought from Sugarplum Sweets. It's this fantastic bakery in town and—"

I stopped talking as he lifted his hand to stop me.

"Get to the point," he said, his voice curt.

"Right. Sorry. I'm not sure what I'm trying to say. Eating

someone's cookie isn't gross. It's actually a very natural thing to do. Though, I don't know why we call it a cookie because it's not like it's shaped like one. And I don't know about you, but I would be worried if it had little chocolate chips—like, what is that?" I laughed nervously, swallowing the rest of my words with a loud gulp when I noticed the unamused smile on his face. "Back to the reason why I'm here… I brought you cookies and hoped that we could sit down and talk for a few minutes."

He studied me so intently that I felt like I was on display. My body flushed as a wave of heat washed over it while his eyes leisurely roamed over my body at a painstakingly slow speed.

"How did you end up stuck to my fence post?"

"Oh. That." I laughed awkwardly again, my anxiety at its full peak now. "Well. I um. I was just checking something."

I pulled my lower lip in between my teeth to keep from continuing. The look he was giving me was fierce, and I would be lying if I said I wasn't scared—and quite turned on—by it.

"Which was?"

I tried to straighten myself as best as I could while mustering up the courage to come clean.

"I came to check on the reindeer."

"Why?"

"Because they're my friends," I scoffed, instantly insulted by his tone.

His eyebrow lifted on its own accord, questioning me.

"I've worked with your grandfather for years, and as the coordinator for Frosty Fest, it was my job to oversee everything—including the reindeer. I've spent a lot of time with them and built friendships."

He lowered his head and shook it as if this was the most absurd thing he'd ever heard.

"What? Why is that so unbelievable to you?"

"Because animals don't have friends. They're not capable of the emotions required to have a *friendship*."

"Uhhh, yeah, they do." I scrunched my face up in disgust. "In fact, they're probably better at it than you are, you old grumpy ass."

My words slipped through my lips before I could stop them.

His head lifted slowly, a splash of humor seeming to light up his eyes before it vanished again.

"And how exactly did you get stuck to the fence post?" he asked, ignoring my comment. "Did you attach yourself to it as a way of protest or something? Like one of those tree-loving people who chain themselves to a tree to keep it from being cut down?"

"No, Mr. Smart Ass. I didn't purposely attach myself to your fence post. I was walking along the wall, trying to get a better look, but I lost my balance. I tried to jump to keep from falling, but as luck would have it, I ended up right on top of the post. Thankfully it didn't hit me in the ass on the way down because that would have hurt." I shivered at the thought and then shivered again when I noticed the change in his eyes when I mentioned my ass.

"I seriously don't understand how this happened." He shook his head and walked around the post, studying each angle. "How did your jacket end up wrapped around it, and why didn't you just unzip it?"

I rubbed my lips together, ignoring the numbness that was now taking over my toes.

"The jacket is too big for me. It's my roommate's. I was heading out the door when I realized I had left mine at work, so I just grabbed it from the hook and left. When I jumped, I must have gotten enough air for it to puff up the jacket, creating the perfect pocket for the post to slide into."

He stepped in front of me and stopped, looking me dead in the eye.

"I know. It sounds ridiculous. Trust me, I tried figuring out a way to free myself before you found me. No one is more embarrassed by this than me."

"I don't think anyone would ever believe me if I told them this happened," he said, shaking his head as he pulled his cell phone out.

"What are you doing?"

"Getting a picture for proof. It would have been better if the cameras were up. Then I could have watched it happen, but this will have to do."

"So you're capturing me in the most humiliating moment of my life for your personal satisfaction? What are you going to do with it?"

"Haven't decided yet." He shrugged as if there were no sense of urgency as a blistering cold gust of wind whipped past us.

"Well, maybe after you decide you can help me off of this thing before I lose a toe? It's freaking cold out here, and some of us don't have the luxury of moving our bodies to stay warm."

"Tell me again why you didn't just unzip the jacket and set yourself free?"

"Because," I said with a heavy sigh. "The zipper is broken. I can't get it to move. I'm literally stuck in here."

He nodded and looked at the post before leaning forward and grabbing my hips.

"What are you doing?" I screeched, eyes wide as my skin sizzled from his touch.

"Setting you free. Are you going to keep yelling at me, or can I get this done before we're both officially stuck out here?"

I nodded, too embarrassed to talk.

"Can you climb under?" he asked, stepping away from me to give me room.

I shook my head.

"I already tried. The post is tight, pinning me against it. I can't get my arms out of the sleeves of the jacket."

"Alright, up and over it is."

I was about to ask what he meant by *up and over*, but then I felt his hands grip my waist and hoist me in the air.

"I need you to trust me and hold on so I don't drop you," he warned, lifting me as if I weighed nothing.

"Okay," I stammered, unsure of how exactly I was supposed to hold on.

"I'm going to lower myself in between your legs so I can get a good grip."

My eyes widened immediately. Before I could react, he was kneeling in front of me, pulling my legs around his neck as he held onto my ass, his face inches away from my pussy.

I closed my eyes as I tried to ignore the thoughts racing through my mind about what a compromising position we were in while he worked to free me from the post. He lifted me higher, freeing the fabric of the jacket from the fence post before stepping away from it. I was still wrapped around his chest like some sort of horny spider monkey, too turned on to get down.

His hands reached up and grabbed my hips, gently lowering me down his body as he set me on my feet again.

"Are you okay?" he asked, eyes narrowing as I stumbled slightly, losing my footing in the snow.

"Yeah. I'm fine. Thanks."

"No problem." He pulled the beanie off his head and shoved a hand through his hair before putting it back on. "I have a lot of questions—like why the hell you're wearing boots like that in the middle of a snowstorm—but I need to get the reindeer moved into the barn before any of that happens."

I rubbed my lips together, wondering if now was the time to press my luck with him.

"I'm more than happy to answer any questions you have if

you want to talk for a few," I offered, falling in step beside him as he stalked off toward the barn across the field from us. "I can help get the reindeer situated if you'd like."

"As much as I want to decline, I don't see you giving me any options with this." He stopped and faced me, his tall frame towering over mine. *He was so good-looking.*

"I'm determined."

"I can see that. I would venture to say careless and reckless, but until I can deal with unpacking all of that, I need to know you're not going to need saving again until I can get inside to deal with you."

"Okay…."

"I'm so going to regret this," he said, more to himself than me as he tipped his head back and closed his eyes. "Go inside the house and wait for me. There's a fresh pot of coffee I started before I came out to rescue you. I'll be in soon."

Giddiness rushed through me at the thought of being inside his home. If I could get just a glimpse into who he was as a person or what he liked, I might be able to find the key to getting him to agree to help me with the reindeer issue.

"Sounds like a plan. I'll fix both of us a cup after I grab the cookies and my purse from the car. How do you like your coffee?"

His nostrils flared as if irritated with the conversation, so I didn't push him. I was making progress and didn't want to ruin it before I got what I needed.

"Black like your soul. Got it," I whispered as he stalked off and left me standing in the middle of the field.

Six
Brody

It was easier to get the reindeer inside the barn and situated before the storm than it was to get rid of the crazy woman who had been stuck to my fence post. Never in a million years would I have believed that could happen, and I still wasn't convinced that she hadn't purposely attached herself to the post as a way to get me to talk to her.

By the time I got back to the house, she was sitting comfortably on my couch with her legs crossed in front of her and a cup of coffee in her hand. On the coffee table in front of her was a plate filled with cookies that I assumed were the ones she kept trying to tell me about earlier—even though we both got distracted by *another* type of cookie, as she called it, as well as a cup of black coffee for me.

"Everything go okay?" she asked, her voice softer than I remembered.

"Yes," I replied curtly as I sat stiffly in the recliner across from her. There was plenty of room for both of us on the couch, but after having her legs wrapped around my head earlier, I needed to distance myself as far away from her as possible. The last thing I needed right now was to let my guard down around her.

"Great. I'm glad you got everything taken care of." She set her cup on the coffee table, using a coaster I had never seen before in my life. Leave it to her to literally make herself at home in a house I was still trying to get used to.

"Thank you for agreeing to take the time to talk with me. I know you don't want to, and I'm sorry that I keep forcing myself upon you, but I really don't have any other choice. Without your help, I'm screwed."

With my help, you could be screwed better. Screwed to the point that your toes curl as you scream my name while I eat the sweet pussy that was sitting in front of my face not that long ago.

"I don't want to be a dick," I answered, my fingers gripping the armrests tightly. "But I can't help you. There's too much that needs my focus right now and giving any of my attention to the Frozen Palooza would mean that I fall behind on what matters."

"Frozen Palooza?" She scrunched her face and looked confused.

"You know, the thing you want the reindeer for," I replied dismissively with a shake of my hand. "My point being that I have stuff here that needs my attention. Repairs that need to be made before I can set up my shop. If I don't get the shop set up, then I can't work. If I can't work, I don't make money. So, I'm sorry, but my priorities don't involve carving out time I don't have right now to help you with whatever this thing is you're planning."

She sat taller, pulling her shoulders back as she tilted her head and studied me.

"What kind of work do you do?"

I shifted in my seat, forcing myself to relax the best I

could. I wasn't big into personal conversations, but the fact that she sat there as if she had all day made me feel like I needed to answer her so we could move on and I could get her out of my house before she got stuck in the storm.

"I'm a welder."

She nodded, smiling, but it wasn't one that reached her eyes. It was a polite, reserved smile that people used when they made small talk like this. It said they cared enough to acknowledge what was said but not enough that they would remember it later. Or, in her case, it was a distracted smile while the wheels in her head started turning.

"What do you weld?"

I ground my teeth together, pushing the frustration out that way instead of taking it out on her. How do you politely tell someone you don't want to make small talk with them? I knew she likely didn't mean any harm by it, but I also wasn't interested in trying to build friendships. I had a goal, and she was delaying me from working toward it by stalling and asking ridiculous questions.

"All sorts of things. Fire pits. Candlestands. Metal yard art."

"Things that would do well somewhere like a festival where local artisans come together and sell their products," she commented softly. "Like Frosty Fest."

"I know what you're doing," I warned, narrowing my eyes at her.

"What?" She fluttered hers, playing innocent. "I'm just pointing out that the *Frosty Fest* would be an ideal marketplace for you to reach new customers. You're new to town, and we don't have any other vendors who sell that type of product. You could literally dominate the market with items we haven't had here before."

"And that benefits you how?"

"Well, it doesn't benefit *me*. It benefits you. It benefits the town. It benefits the people from neighboring towns who choose to come here to take part in the festival and do some holiday shopping."

"I hate to break it to you, but I have no interest in participating." I stood up, making it clear that the conversation was over.

"If you just—"

"My answer is no. Thank you for coming all the way out here and bringing cookies, but this will be the last time we have this conversation. I expect you'll be able to respect the boundaries I'm setting and that I won't find you wandering around my property again."

She reached down and grabbed her purse before standing up. I hated the hurt look on her face but I couldn't give in just because I was attracted to her. I had a plan and needed to stick to it. I didn't have the time or the luxury of getting caught up in a personal relationship right now.

"Thank you for your time," she said quietly, lowering her head as she walked past me to the front door.

I opened it and stepped to the side, not believing my eyes as a cloud of snow blew past us, the wind howling in the distance.

She gasped and jumped back, both of our eyes widening as

we took in the scene in front of us. In a matter of minutes, enough snow had accumulated, making it impossible to spot her SUV.

32

Seven

Jasmin

"I'll be fine," I shouted over my shoulder, knowing Brody couldn't hear me over the wind howling past us as I sunk deeper into the snow.

There was no way in hell I was going to be stuck in the middle of nowhere with him. I was determined to comb every inch of the ranch until I could find my SUV and get the hell out of there. He had made it abundantly clear that he didn't want to be around me, so I was going to give him what he wanted.

"Why are you being so difficult?" he growled, suddenly behind me as strong hands gripped my waist and stopped me.

"I'm not. I'm trying to get out of here before I get stuck with the grumpiest ass I've ever met!" I shouted, my eyes blinking rapidly to see through the snow that was falling between us.

"It's a little too late for that, Princess."

He stood in front of me, towering over me to where I had to tilt my head back to see him.

"Don't call me that."

"Why not?"

"Because I'm not a princess. I'm a strong, independent woman who doesn't need a man to—"

Before I could finish my sentence, he leaned forward and grabbed me, tossing me over his shoulder as he stomped back to the house.

"Put me down, you big bully!" I pounded my fists against his back, trying to get him to listen.

A few minutes later, I was greeted by warmth as I watched the door slam shut behind us. He bent down, placing me on the rug in the entryway, eyes boring into me.

"I told you to let me go." I placed my hands on my hips and glared at him.

"And I told you I'm busy and don't have time for this shit."

"Which is why I was trying to get out of your hair," I objected, throwing my hands in the air in frustration.

"How the hell do you think you're going anywhere in that? You can't even see your car, let alone the road." He pointed a finger toward the large window, proving his point as a blanket of white fell outside.

"I told you—I'm determined. I would find a way."

"And then I would have to waste more time I don't have digging your body out of the snow when you got stuck and froze to death."

"So what am I supposed to do now?" My irritation was growing thicker as we stood inches apart, staring each other down.

"It seems we're stuck together for a few days, whether we

like it or not."

"No." I shook my head vehemently. "There has to be another option. Something—*anything* other than this."

"Sorry, *Princess*, this is what happens when you go snooping around places you're not supposed to be. Seems luck wasn't on your side, and now you're stuck here until the storm passes."

He pulled off his jacket and hung it on the coat rack beside the door before breezing past me.

"You've got to be kidding me," I grumbled, tossing my head back and closing my eyes.

"That's the same thing I said when you started talking about the Frozen Palooza." He winked as if I would find him funny.

I didn't. He was downright infuriating, and I wanted nothing more than to punch him in the dick and steal his reindeer.

"Frosty Fest," I snarled, hands planted firmly on my hips.

"Tomayto- tomahto."

"No," I growled, shaking my head as I followed him into the kitchen. "You don't get to dismiss it as something stupid that you make fun of. Frosty Fest is an amazing event that helps hundreds of people every year. You don't get to discount it just because you're some cranky grinch who hates Christmas, Brody."

He opened the refrigerator and then closed it, locking his eyes on me.

"How do you know my name?"

My eyes fluttered rapidly as I tried to figure out where that came from.

"What?"

"How do you know my name? I didn't tell you."

He leaned against the counter, arms folded over his chest as he studied me.

My face heated with embarrassment, knowing I was going to have to come clean about how I knew so much about him.

"It's a small town. Everyone knows everyone's name," I countered, trying my best to appear unphased by his question.

"I don't know yours."

"Well, that, my friend, is because you didn't bother to ask." I pointed my finger at him, spinning it in circles as I tried to stay focused. "I don't want to keep bringing it up, but your manners kind of suck. I mean, who has several conversations with someone and doesn't even know their name? Sheesh." I looked away before I made more embarrassing noises, my blush already showing how uncomfortable I was to be put on the spot.

"Yeah, well, we haven't had an actual conversation until today. You just keep showing up and forcing yourself on me."

My jaw dropped at his words.

"I did NOT force myself on you," I objected, stepping

closer to him as I poked a finger at his chest. *Man, that's hard.* "I never asked you to hoist me in the air and put your face right by my lady bits. You did all of that yourself. If anything, *you* might be the one forcing yourself onto *me*."

I stepped back, needing distance between us to keep the fog from taking over my head. There was this pull I felt every time I got too close to him, and even though I was curious about it, I also knew I would be the one to get burned.

"I had to lift you to get you unstuck from the post—which you wouldn't have gotten stuck on had you not been forcing yourself onto my property and looking around when you weren't invited."

My mouth opened to contest what he was saying, but the words wouldn't come out.

"Do you eat meat?" he asked, suddenly changing the subject as he opened the fridge again.

"Meat?"

Was he subtly flirting with me? Was meat code word for something else? I had no idea what he was packing, but I could possibly be interested in checking out his sausage—if that was what he meant.

"Steak, specifically."

I shook my head, feeling like my brain cells were depleting quickly.

"For dinner," he continued, unamused. "I'm making steak and baked potatoes for dinner. Do you want some, or are you one of those who only eat organic plant stuff?"

I took a deep breath in, hoping the oxygen would restore

my ability to think clearly around this man.

"Yes, I eat steak."

"How do you like it cooked?"

He set the package of meat on the counter and looked over his shoulder as he waited for me to answer.

"Medium."

"Alright. I'll let you know when supper is ready."

I shifted my weight, unsure of what to do with myself now.

"Do you need any help?" I offered.

"Nope."

I nodded my head, hating how uncomfortable it was right now.

"If you have a shovel, I can go out and start—"

"Do you have a death wish?" he snapped, turning on me so quickly I had to take a step back.

"Maybe?" I mean, where he was involved, it might be better at this point.

He stepped in front of me, invading my space again.

"I don't want you to be stuck here any more than you want to be stuck here. But I've already told you that trying to leave in this storm is stupid. Now, I don't know if you just have a hard time accepting no as an answer, but I don't have time to play these games with you. If you want to be helpful, go find something for us to watch on TV and take off those so-called boots before you trip and break your ankle. I don't need anything else to worry about right now."

I stepped back and looked down at my feet.

"They're not stupid. They're cute."

"They're ridiculous to be wearing in this weather, and you're just asking for trouble in them."

"Fine," I said with a dramatic sigh and roll of the eyes. "I'll take them off, you big grump."

"Thank you."

I turned to walk away but stopped and spun around to look at him.

"It *does* have manners!" I squealed, clapping my hands for added effect.

He glared and then turned back to the stove to prepare dinner.

<u>Eight</u>
Brody

"Hey… you…" I struggled to remember her name, even though she had just told me during dinner. "Girl with the ridiculous boots—get in here."

I stood beside my bed with a handful of blankets in my arms as she walked in, eyes narrowed in disapproval.

"Girl with the ridiculous boots? Are you kidding me?"

"Sorry. I forgot your name. Anyway, the bed is ready, and I have some extra blankets if you need them."

"My name is Jasmin. And I'm not sleeping in your bed. I already told you I'll take the couch."

She extended her hand to take a blanket but frowned when I refused to pass one to her.

"And I told you the couch sucks and you're not sleeping on it."

"Yeah, well, I'm not sharing a bed with you. Give me the blanket, and I'll sleep on the floor."

"Like hell you will."

She tilted her head and stared at me.

"We might not have gotten off to the best start, but there

is no way in hell I'm allowing you to sleep on the floor. Nor are you sleeping on the couch. So you can either tell me which side of the bed you want, or I'll decide for you. Either way, you're sleeping in here tonight."

"You think you can just boss me around, don't you?"

"I'm not trying to boss you around. I'm tired and want to go to bed, but *someone* keeps making everything more difficult than it needs to be. It's a bed—it's not like we have to touch or make anything more out of it."

"Yes, but it's *your* bed. I'm not just going to climb into your bed because you tell me to. I may not have a choice about being stuck here, but I have one about where I sleep."

"What's wrong with it being *my* bed?"

"I don't like sleeping in other people's beds. End of story."

"Then consider it like a hotel," I offered, my patience growing thinner by the second.

"I don't like hotels either."

"You're impossible. You do know that, right?"

"Just because I don't bend over and do exactly what you say doesn't make me impossible."

"Okay, then explain to me while we're still arguing over *where* you're going to sleep instead of actually getting some sleep."

"I told you I would sleep in the living room, but *you* keep fighting with me about it."

"Because that isn't a decent place to sleep!" I bellowed,

hating that I was raising my voice to her.

It wasn't that my furniture was subpar or anything, but it was my grandfather's and had seen better days. Getting new furniture was on my list of things to do, but it sat at the bottom of eight hundred million other things that needed my attention first.

"Fine," she said through gritted teeth. "Just tell me what side of the bed you want me on."

I rolled my eyes, trying to rein in my frustration.

"How about the left side? It's closest to the bathroom."

"Oh, and because I'm a girl, I automatically need to be close to the bathroom? How incredibly sexist of you."

I dropped the blankets to the bed and scrubbed a hand down my face. She was going to be the death of me. Hell, this was probably her plan all along—drive me crazy to the point she killed me and could steal the reindeer for her stupid Frozen Palooza.

"I'm just trying to be a nice guy and make things more comfortable for you," I replied sternly, my eyes finally opening to see her walking across the room to look inside the bathroom.

"Thank you. I'm sorry for being *difficult*. This wasn't how I expected to spend my night—just like you didn't either. I appreciate you offering me a place to stay until the storm passes."

"You're welcome."

I set a stack of blankets on her side of the bed and then went to the kitchen for a drink of water while giving her time to get settled. I had also set out a T-shirt and a pair of sweats for her since I figured she wasn't going to want to sleep in the outfit she had on. It went fine with the pointy boots she had on earlier, but the tight, shimmery pants and low-cut shirt didn't look comfortable to try to sleep in.

By the time I got back to the room, she was under the covers and facing the bathroom so I couldn't see her face. I grabbed a pair of joggers from the closet and changed before climbing onto my side of the bed. It felt weird to be sharing the space with someone else, but I tried to ignore that as I forced myself to get some rest. Tomorrow would be an early day with a mountain of a list of things to do.

Nine

Jasmin

I woke up to the smell of coffee floating through the air. I had slept better than I imagined, though I had gotten up a few times, restless about being stuck sleeping beside a stranger.

Brody seemed nice enough not to try to murder me in his sleep, but then again, he was irritated enough with me that I wouldn't blame him for trying. I wasn't trying to be difficult, but I hadn't expected to be put in the situation to begin with.

I got up and used the restroom, secretly thankful that he had been thoughtful enough to give me that side of the bed. I had been up a few times throughout the night, and it was nice not having to go far since I didn't know my way around his house yet.

He was in the kitchen, sitting at the dining room table with a cup of coffee in one hand and a book in the other. For whatever reason, it shocked me to see him sitting there, reading for pleasure. He didn't strike me as the type that found pleasure in much.

"Good morning," I said, trying to muster as much friendliness to my tone as possible.

"Morning."

I pulled my shoulders down, trying not to start the day with more tension than there already was.

I debated whether or not to help myself to the pot of coffee that was calling my name. There was a cup sitting on the counter beside it, which I assumed meant it was for me, given he was already drinking his. But still, I wasn't ready to come in and make myself at home.

"Coffee is ready, and breakfast is on the island. Help yourself," he said as if reading my mind without looking up from his book.

"Thank you."

I took a few minutes to fix myself a cup of coffee, hating that nothing would compare to one of Sam's lattes right now. I was officially addicted to Sugarplum Lattes, just like everyone else in town. Sam denied putting anything in there other than the basic ingredients, but I was convinced he used some sort of drug to keep us needing our fix.

There was a plate sitting on the island beside the trays of food, which felt oddly thoughtful for the grumpy man sitting at the table. I picked it up and added some scrambled eggs and a few strips of bacon to my plate, not wanting to take too much.

"I've already eaten. Take what you want."

How the fuck was he doing that? Did he have eyes in the back of his head, or was he somehow infiltrating my brain?

I added a few pancakes and a piece of toast, smiling when I realized it was more than what I typically ate for breakfast. Most days I was busy from the moment I opened my eyes and didn't have time for much other than stuffing a protein bar down my throat in between meetings.

I grabbed my coffee and plate, then stopped, not wanting to invade his space at the table.

He closed his book and stood up, pushing his chair back under the table before giving me a nod and leaving the room. This man was more confusing than eleventh-grade algebra. For me being in his way and making things harder for him, he sure was going out of his way to make me comfortable in his home.

I sat down on the other side of the table and took a sip of coffee. It was quiet, which was surprisingly peaceful compared to the constant noise and stimulation I was used to working at the mall. Since Sugarplum Falls was such a small town, we hosted the majority of our events at the mall because it had the space we needed and helped to boost sales at the stores by driving more traffic there. And since I was the town's event planner—including Frosty Fest—it just made sense that my office was at the mall, where all the action took place.

As I ate, I scrolled through my emails on my phone, deciding which ones needed my attention first. It was still technically a workday, even if I was stranded in the middle of nowhere until the stupid storm passed. With less than two weeks away from Frosty Fest, my to-do list was overflowing with stuff that I needed to get taken care of.

I replied to a few emails and marked some as urgent so I could focus on them as soon as I got back to town. I had no idea how long it would take for the storm to pass, but given the amount of snow that fell last night, I wasn't feeling too hopeful that it would be soon.

I finished my food and put my plate in the dishwasher before packing up the rest on the island and putting it in the fridge. I hadn't seen Brody in a while but didn't want to be in his way any more than I already was by asking him what he wanted to do with the leftovers. I also didn't want to just make myself at home, so I went back to the table and decided that would be where I would work from for the day. I grabbed my purse, dug out the notepad and pen I kept on me at all times, and started going through my list for the day.

Before I could get through the first few items, my phone rang.

"This is Jasmin," I answered, tucking the phone between my ear and shoulder as I made another note on my pad about doubling the cookie order I was placing with Andi.

"You don't even look at your caller ID before you answer it, do you?" Sam teased, bringing a smile to my lips.

"I just went into work mode, so I have blinders on already." I laughed, leaning back in the chair as I looked around the room, wondering where Brody was. "What's up?"

"Well, you didn't come in for your morning fix, so I was calling to check on you. I know you usually get the brunt of the storm where you live, so I wanted to see if you needed help getting out today. It's been slow this morning, so I can jet over there and clear your driveway if you need me to."

"Thank you for the offer. That's very sweet of you, but I'm not at home."

"Oh. Yeah, no worries. I just thought since you hadn't been in yet…"

"I'm actually stuck at Brody's ranch." I lowered my voice, making sure to speak directly into the phone so Sam could hear me.

"I'm sorry—you're where?"

"You heard it right the first time. I came by yesterday to try to get him to change his mind about the reindeer and ended up getting stuck to a fence post—which is a long story I don't want to get into right now. But the short story is that the storm moved in before I could get out, and he's acting like an uncivilized caveman who is forcing me to stay here until it passes."

"I'm not sure what to do with all of that," Sam said with a laugh. "I feel like we should get Aiden on the phone since this is definitely heavy cocktails bar talk level of gossip."

"Trust me, it's anticlimactic. I mean, he did have his head between my legs for a few minutes, but neither of us got any pleasure out of that."

I winced when I realized my words *after* I said them. But that was the thing about Sam; he was like talking to your closest girlfriend and didn't care how raunchy the conversation ended up being. He never crossed that line with our friendship or made it uncomfortable.

"Yup, this is definitely bar talk that we'll need to save for Aiden. How long do you think you'll be out there?"

I glanced out the window, noticing that the snow had started again.

"I have no idea. I can't see my car at this point, and crotchety ass Mr. Caveman won't let me go try to dig it out."

"That's because I don't feel like having to save you again, *Princess*," Brody said from behind me, scaring the shit out of me.

"Holy shit! Where did you come from?" I asked, covering the mouthpiece of my phone with my hand as Sam laughed on the other end.

"This *is* my house and I do live here." He looked at me over his shoulder as he strolled past the table and refilled his cup of coffee.

I shook my head and gave him a dirty look before returning my attention to Sam.

"Thanks for checking on me, Sam. I appreciate it." I made sure to say his name loud enough for Brody to hear— just in case it might make him worried that I was talking to another man. It wasn't like Brody was attracted or interested in me, but still, it didn't hurt to have him know that someone else cared enough to check on me, just in case he decided to kill me after all. And if I had to bet on it, Sam could whoop Brody's ass. "I need to get going but I'll let you know when I'm able to get back to Sugarplum Falls."

"Sounds good, though I'm sure it'll be obvious when you're knocking people down in line to get your gingerbread latte."

"That was *one* time," I hissed. "And those tourists wouldn't move to the side while they looked at the menu. It's just common sense to move aside for those who actually know what they want."

"Well, be sure to keep that in mind while you're stuck there. It also doesn't hurt to allow yourself to be open to other things you may not realize you want."

"Sam," I said with a heavy sigh. "It is way too early in the morning for your metaphorical riddles."

"It's not a riddle." He laughed. "I'm just saying, you know what you think you want, but don't be so close-minded that you don't allow yourself to be open to things you didn't know you wanted."

"It's all about the reindeer. Got it."

"That's not what I meant."

"Well, I guess I'm choosing to hear what I want to hear."

"Sounds about right. Take care and if you need anything, call. Aiden and I will figure out a way to come rescue you."

"You make it sound like you're both some knights in shining armor," I teased playfully, only looking up when I felt Brody's eyes on me from across the room.

"I guess that would make *you* the princess who needs saving," Sam offered.

I felt my skin prickle as I thought about how much I hated it when Brody called me that. It was going to be a long, trying day being stuck here with him.

52

<u>Ten</u>
Brody

I sat on the couch, watching the twelve o'clock news to see when this storm was supposed to pass. It wasn't just the unexpected company that was getting to me; it was the wasted days not being able to get outside to do the work I needed to. I knew when I moved back to Sugarplum Falls that the winters would be brutal; I was just hopeful that I would still be able to work through them so it didn't set me back too far.

Crazy boot lady had sat at the kitchen table for most of the day, taking phone calls and scribbling notes on the worn-out notepad in front of her. I tried not to eavesdrop too much on her calls, but I couldn't help but laugh when I heard how many holly-jolly catastrophes she was dealing with. For it being the most wonderful time of the year, it sure seemed like a disaster from an outsider looking in.

I turned off the TV and went to the kitchen to make a sandwich for lunch. It seemed luck had been on my side yesterday with me getting into town and back before the storm hit. I had plenty of groceries, plus I had stocked up on meat and household essentials to last me for a few months.

"Hey, Princess, do you want a sandwich?" I asked once she removed her phone from her ear and set it on the table.

She looked up at me from under thick, dark eyelashes, her eyes a moody mixture of shades of brown.

"I told you not to call me that."

"Yeah, well, I figured it's better than *hey, you.*"

"Or you could call me by my name."

"That would mean that I actually stopped to bother with remembering it. We're only stuck together for a few days, *Princess.* No need to get so formal with each other. Once the roads are cleared, I'll dig your car out, and you can go on your merry way."

"God, you're such an asshole. I should have known, given you were described as a grinch. But still, I held out hope that they were wrong."

"And who exactly is *they*?" I questioned, leaning against the island as I pinned her with a look. It didn't surprise me that people in town were talking about me. That's what happens in a small town. But what bothered me was *where* she was getting her information.

"The townspeople," she replied dismissively with a wave of her hand. "But it doesn't matter because I can confirm from firsthand experience that they're right. You are the epitome of a grinch."

"Well, thank you for the compliment." I winked, quickly earning a scowl from her.

"That's not a compliment!" She threw her hands in the air and shook her head. "A compliment is you have nice eyes or you have a radiant smile that brightens the room."

"Well, thanks for those as well. Aren't you just full of

compliments today?"

She sighed heavily, my attempt at humor clearly rubbing her the wrong way. *Maybe she needed me to rub her the right way. That might lighten her mood a bit.*

"You're impossible."

"So you've said." I turned and opened the fridge, grabbing the stuff to make sandwiches. "Now, do you want a sandwich or not?"

"Are you making it?" she fired back, getting up and joining me at the island.

"Do you want me to?"

"No. I think I'd rather eat poison than have you cook for me."

I didn't bother to remind her that she had gladly eaten the steak and baked potato I fixed for dinner last night or that she devoured breakfast this morning. It was like she had gotten a fresh dose of hatred for me, and I kinda liked going back and forth, riling her up.

"That can be arranged." I pulled out two slices of bread and slapped them down onto the plate. I noticed the way she jumped slightly and fought back the grin tugging at my lips as I noticed her eyes fixated on what I was doing. The sound wasn't intended, but it still very much sounded like a spank.

I had seen a few social media videos that my cousin sent to me of this guy who cooks, but everything he does looks incredibly sexual. Taking a cue from him now that I had her attention, I made sure to give her a show. It wasn't like we had anything better to do, given we were stuck together for who knew how long. Plus, she could use something to help her lighten up a bit.

I opened the jar of mayonnaise, and then, instead of using a knife, I inserted two fingers— yup, those two. I moved them around, slowly stirring the top layer as my fingers got coated. I felt her eyes on me as she watched—likely wondering if I was out of my fucking mind. I was.

I grabbed a piece of bread and held it in one palm while I smothered it with the mayonnaise on my fingers, rubbing it down the middle before spreading my fingers to get to the sides. I could feel the tension building between us, my dick already starting to strain against my jeans. I set the bread down on the plate and then sucked my fingers clean, looking up to lock eyes with her as she watched my tongue work strategically.

Next, I grabbed a pack of deli lunch meat and slowly slid the zipper open, too invested in this to stop now. With my eyes still locked on her, I reached inside and grabbed the meat, gripping it tightly before pulling a few slices free and slapping them down onto the bread. She jumped again, and I couldn't help but wonder if the sound mimicking spanking turned her on. It sure seemed to, which made me picture just how nice her ass would look with a red handprint on it from me.

I opened another pack of lunch meat and did the same, loving her reaction as I slapped the ham down on top of the turkey. At this point, I wished I had more meat to keep this party going. I opened the package of cheese and slowly peeled one off before adding it to the sandwich.

Then, to top it all off, I grabbed the bottle of mustard, turned it upside down, and smacked it with the palm of my hand. Her eyes widened as she chewed on her lower lip, taking it all in. I lifted the bottle over the sandwich and started to squeeze, loving the opening I'd been given when an air bubble got caught and forced some of it to splatter.

"Looks like she's a squirter," I said nonchalantly, her eyes moving up to meet mine. "But that's okay, I don't mind. What fun is it if it's not messy?"

I was more than just playing with fire. I was taking a box of matches and gallons of gasoline to a dry forest during a lightning storm.

With her eyes still on me, I reached down with those same two fingers and spread the mustard before licking it off.

"So, do you want a sandwich?" I asked, ignoring how gruff my voice sounded.

"A sandwich?" she questioned, her voice suddenly high-pitched. "That's not a sandwich. That's porn."

My smirk spread across my face as I studied her, wondering what she was into, given how invested she had become in my silly little experiment.

"Trust me, that's not porn. But if this really turns you on, you can watch me eat. I really, really love *eating*." I added the other piece of bread to the top, then lifted it to my mouth and took a huge bite. Some of the mustard got on the side of my mouth, so I deliberately swiped my tongue out to lick it off.

Her face was flushed with the prettiest color as heat washed over her.

"I need fresh air," she muttered, turning away from me and heading to the door before she stopped. She knew as well as I did that she wasn't going anywhere with the amount of snow that was currently piled against the door. Without saying a word, she turned around and went straight to the bathroom, slamming the door behind her.

I considered making her a sandwich but had no idea what she liked. I knew it was already crossing the line with what I had just done, but in all fairness, it wasn't my fault. I didn't ask her to get stuck here, and I couldn't deny that I was attracted to her.

I sat down on the couch with my plate resting beside me as I picked up the remote to turn on the TV. Before I could, I heard a faint noise coming from the bathroom. Despite knowing it was wrong, I got up and quietly walked over so I could hear it better.

From the other side of the door I heard soft moaning.

Was she seriously masturbating in my bathroom right now? I wasn't upset about it in the least—if anything, I was jealous that I wasn't the one in there giving her pleasure. The way she sounded made my cock harden again, desperate to hear more.

"Fuck, Brody," she moaned quietly, though loud enough I could hear her from the other side.

I raised my eyebrows in surprise, nodding my head in agreement. So, she was thinking about me to get off. That was a problem I could easily deal with if she would let me. I could make her feel better than anything she was doing in there right now. I could give her the best orgasm of her life before fucking her senseless.

Sensing that she was done and getting ready to come out soon, I retreated back to the couch, turned on the TV, and pretended I hadn't just heard her coming to the thought of me.

60

Eleven

Jasmin

I masturbated in his bathroom.

Not even five minutes after watching him make a stupid sandwich and I was ready to hump the arm of the couch just to get some relief.

What the hell was that?

I wasn't the kind of girl who was so hard up that I pleasured myself to thoughts of a guy fingering a jar of mayonnaise—which, by the way, was pretty fucking hot. Never in my life have I wanted to be something as gross as mayonnaise until now.

I tried to be quiet, but there was so much built-up tension that I couldn't help but moan and cry out his name as the stars blinded me from such an intense orgasm. I ignored the thoughts of what would happen if *he* had been the one to touch me instead of just imagining it. Would he have gotten me off just as good? Part of me knew that it wouldn't be just as good—it would be better. He was the kind of man who, once you experienced what he could do, nothing else would ever satisfy you again. But that wasn't anything I had to worry about because the likelihood of Brody ever touching me was slim to none.

After the little bathroom incident, I tried to distract myself with work by planting my ass in the chair at the kitchen table and keeping my head down. I ignored the way the energy seemed to crackle between us every time he walked by. It was like there was this raw electricity, and I was bound to get zapped.

"You need to eat," he said, plopping a sandwich down on a plate beside me. "I didn't know what you liked, so it's just plain with meat and cheese. You can find whatever you need in the fridge."

I nodded, afraid to look him in the eyes after what I had done.

Without any warning, his finger reached below my chin and lifted my head so I had to look at him.

"If you want me to finger some mayo for you, all you have to do is ask. I already told you I don't mind it being messy."

I licked my lips instinctively as I thought about the mustard squirting and his comment about loving to eat.

"I don't like mayo," I said softly, my voice barely above a whisper.

Humor danced in his eyes as his finger continued to hold my chin.

"Well, if you need anything, you know where to find it."

He finally released his hold on me and then walked off. I watched as he pulled his jacket and beanie on, then went out the front door, closing it behind him.

The snow had stopped, and according to the news he was watching earlier, the worst of the storm had already moved through. This was technically good news, but since I was stuck out in the middle of nowhere, that didn't mean I would be able to get out of here anytime soon.

Before I could process everything that had just happened, my phone rang. I looked down to see Andi's name on the caller ID as I swiped to answer it.

"Hey," I said, a little too breathlessly.

"Hi. Everything okay?"

"Yeah. I'm fine. Why do you ask?"

"I talked to Sam, and he told me you were stranded at Brody's place. Then you answer, sounding all out of breath…"

"Oh. Yeah. I'm stuck here. It's fine, though."

"Why are you being weird? Did you murder him, and now you're trying to hide the body, and that's why you sound out of breath?"

"No! Andi!" I laughed, leaning back in my chair. "Why would you say that?"

"Well, I know how badly you want those reindeer, and Sam said that it sounded like you two were already bickering. I guess I just assumed you were doing whatever had to be done to keep Frosty Fest afloat."

"While I would technically do anything to keep Frosty Fest afloat, murder isn't high on the list."

"Okay, but that still doesn't explain the breathl—"

I closed my eyes and waited as she finished processing what she was about to say.

"Oh my God! Jasmin! You slept with him? Please tell me that it's just wild, crazy, stuck together during a blizzard, and you have nothing better to do sex and not that you're sleeping with him to get the reindeer."

"Do you really think I would go to that extreme?"

"For the reindeer? Yeah, I kinda do. I mean, I saw him in line at Waldon's yesterday when I ran in to get some stuff, and he's not bad to look at. But I don't want you selling yourself short just to get the reindeer."

"That's not at all what is happening," I muttered, looking outside to make sure he was still there and hadn't snuck back in. "We haven't had sex."

"But you want to."

I tapped my fingers on the table, knowing she was right but not wanting to admit it.

"Why don't you just make a move on him?" she suggested, pulling my thoughts back to the conversation and away from the sandwich porn.

"No way. I'm not even interested in him. He did some freaky shit with a sandwich, and it just got me flustered. That's all."

"Freaky shit to a sandwich? Like he used his dick to make a sausage sandwich or something?"

"No!" I laughed, shaking my head. "He didn't have his dick out."

"Okay, I'm lost."

"He was making a sandwich for himself, and I was

watching. I don't know why, so don't bother with asking. Anyway, he just randomly decided to make it the most sensual sandwich-making experience in the world, and it left me a little flustered."

"What did he do?"

"Well, for starters, instead of using a knife like a normal human being, he stuck his fingers in the jar of mayonnaise and practically fingered it before spreading it on the bread. Then he sucked his fingers clean, and I know he was flicking the tips of them with his tongue just to get to me."

"Oh my!" Andi was giggling on the other end, which helped lighten my mood.

"Then he kept slapping things down. The meat. The cheese. The bread. Soooo much slapping, Andi. And every time he did it, I couldn't help but imagine him spanking me as he took me from behind."

"Shit. That's hot."

"It was. And then he put mustard on, and you know how sometimes air bubbles get stuck when you're trying to get it out?"

"Yeah, it splatters everywhere."

"Exactly! Well, it did that, and he made a comment about it being a squirter and that he didn't mind messy. Then he continued to tell me how much he loves to *eat*."

"Whew. Now you're getting me all hot and bothered," she said quietly. "No, I'm not talking about you. Get back to work." Her voice was muffled with the last sentence, clearly not talking to me as she sounded like she was trying to cover the mouthpiece.

"So, what are you going to do about this?" she asked. "You guys apparently have some sizzling chemistry, and he wouldn't be doing this if he wasn't attracted to you. By the sounds of it, you're equally attracted to him."

"I kinda went into his bathroom and *took care of things*," I whispered into the phone, embarrassed to admit it out loud.

"While he was there?"

"Yes! He was literally in the other room, and Andi, I came so hard I saw stars. STARS! No one has ever made me come that hard before, and he didn't even touch me. I just pictured him making that stupid sandwich, and I was done."

"So why don't you tell him you want to be the next sandwich he eats?"

"I can't do that!"

"Why not?"

"Because what if this is all one-sided? What if he's not interested in anything like that? I mean, he's the biggest asshole I've ever met, so it wouldn't surprise me if he were just doing this to mess with me since I got stranded here and forced myself into his space."

"I doubt that it is. I know he's grumpy and all, but I can't imagine he would make those comments unless he were willing to act on them."

"I don't know. But one thing is for certain—he better stop because I feel like a ticking time bomb, already ready to explode again."

"See, tell him about your little problem and ask if he wants to help fix it. You guys can work out a little friends-with-benefits situation while you're there. Win-win for both of you."

"We would have to be friends in order for that to work."

"Okay, an enemies with benefits situation. It doesn't really matter what you call it as long as he helps alleviate some of that pressure for you."

"I would rather hump the couch," I admitted. "Or a pillow with his face on it."

"Jasmin!" She gasped. "You're such a little freak."

She laughed, making me laugh with her.

"But now I know what to get you for Christmas," she teased. "A nice new pillow with his face on it and maybe some new toys from Dark Vibes."

"They seriously have the best stuff."

"Alright, well, I gotta get going. We've got a line out the door, and Zach is heading to lunch. I just wanted to make sure you were okay—which clearly, you're doing just fine. If you need anything, let us know."

"Thanks. I appreciate it."

I hung up the phone and set it on the table as I contemplated ordering myself a new Dark Vibes toy.

Twelve
Brody

I rolled over, feeling restless as crazy boot lady snored beside me. It was hard sharing my bed with someone since I hadn't done that in who knew how long. But it was even harder after hearing her moan my name earlier in the bathroom as she got herself off.

I closed my eyes and tried to picture sheep, but all I could see was her. Her beautiful brown eyes and narrow cheeks that turned the prettiest shade of pink when she was embarrassed. Curves that begged to be touched and an ass that I wanted to spank.

My dick began to strain against the joggers I was wearing, already getting aroused by thoughts of her. It wouldn't take much to get off tonight, and maybe that would be the cure to getting some sleep. Maybe I just needed to get rid of the mounting tension that was constantly spreading to my groin as I struggled not to come on to her.

I pulled the blankets off of me, ready to get out of bed, when I stopped.

She had rolled onto her back, her eyes still closed as her hand drifted below the waistband of the sweats she borrowed from me. I wanted to give her privacy and look away because there was no way in hell she knew what she was doing right now. But I couldn't.

I sat there, my eyes glued to the way the fabric pulled down enough to show her hip bone and the top of her black panties. Her back arched as a soft smile spread across her face while her fingers played with her pussy.

"Ahhh, Brody," she whimpered, causing my dick to harden more.

I was rock hard, my balls starting to ache with need.

Her hand slipped lower, pulling the fabric down with it, exposing her pussy to me as I watched her fingers glisten as they dipped inside.

"Make me come. Please."

I pinched my eyes closed and pulled in a deep breath through my nose, reminding myself that she was asleep and not literally inviting me to touch her.

"Eat my pussy. Make me squirt. Fuck me."

I reached down and gripped the sheets, struggling to stay in control. I wanted nothing more than to whip my cock out and jack off to her getting herself off. But the last thing I wanted was for her to wake up to that image.

"I'm so close. I'm so close. Please, Brody. I'm so close. Make me come," she begged, squirming on the bed as her fingers moved faster.

Then suddenly, she stopped, and her eyes fluttered open. She took a few seconds to look around before spotting me sitting on the bed beside her. Then she looked down, noticed her hand still in her panties, and yanked it out.

"Oh my God. Please tell me you didn't see what I think you did," she muttered, sitting up and bringing her knees up to her chest, resting her head on them.

"I didn't see anything you didn't want me to see."

"Brody," she groaned. "Why didn't you wake me?"

I shrugged, not that she could see it. What was I supposed to say? It was too fucking arousing for me to think about anything other than giving her the orgasm she was so close to getting.

"I don't know," I admitted sheepishly.

"This day could not get any more embarrassing. Now you know what I sound like when I'm…"

I shifted on the bed, turning to face her even though she still refused to look at me.

"Technically, I already knew what you sounded like when you moan my name."

I knew it was a dick move to bring up what she had done earlier, but I wanted her to talk to me about this. The last thing I wanted was to keep having these giant elephants in the room that we had to try to avoid while she was staying with me. The storm might have passed, but it would still be days before anyone got the roads clear enough to get out of here.

Her head whipped up as she pierced me with a look.

"What are you talking about?"

"Earlier, when you snuck off to the bathroom to get yourself off after I made a sandwich. I heard you."

Her eyes bulged out of her head, but thankfully she didn't

look away this time.

"Okay. That solves it," she said, pushing the covers the rest of the way off of her as she swung her legs over the side of the bed.

"Solves what?"

"I can't stay here any longer. I've embarrassed myself enough, so it's time to leave."

"And where exactly do you think you're going to go at two in the morning?"

"I don't know. I'll go dig my car out and sleep in there until the sun is up."

"Stop being ridiculous."

"I'm not. I'm mortified that you've heard me moan your stupid name and that you just caught whatever that was. Which, by the way, I don't need you telling me. I can embarrass myself enough by guessing what I was doing."

I got up and walked around the bed, stopping her from leaving.

"Why are you embarrassed?"

She narrowed her eyes at me and then looked away.

"Seriously, why are you embarrassed?"

"Why wouldn't I be? It would be like you jacking off and moaning my name for me to hear or see."

"I have no problem doing that if it turns you on."

I hated that it was dark in the room because I would bet

money on how red her cheeks were from that comment.

"I didn't say it would turn me on. I simply said that anyone caught masturbating would be embarrassed."

"I don't agree."

"Of course you wouldn't. You purposely disagree with me just to get under my skin."

"I do not."

"You're doing it right now!"

"Okay, okay," I said, taking a step back to give her some space. "I am not trying to rile you up. I just don't agree that masturbation should be something to be embarrassed about. Honestly, the thought of you touching yourself is hotter than fuck, and I would watch that over porn any day. Second, masturbation is a natural thing. People do it all the time. Sometimes, our bodies need a release that no one else can give us. It's nothing to be ashamed of."

She seemed to give it some thought but still refused to look at me.

"Do you want me to finish you off?" I offered.

I knew it was bold and brazen of me, but at the same time, I knew she didn't come from touching herself in her sleep. I could imagine the discomfort she was feeling because I was feeling it, too.

"What?"

"Do you want me to bring you to climax? I know you didn't come just now, and your body is probably uncomfortable from all that build-up, only to have nothing release it."

She shook her head and then looked up at me.

"You can't be serious."

"Dead."

She rolled her eyes.

"I don't see what the problem is. We're both adults. If we're both consenting, then why not do something that makes you feel better? It doesn't always have to be tied to a relationship. Sometimes, it can be just sex and nothing else."

"I'm not having sex with you."

"I didn't say you have to. I offered to get you off. You can pick how. I can finger you until you squirt, or I can eat you out so you come on my face. If you decide you want to have sex, I can fuck you at the right angle to make my cock get you there. There are endless possibilities."

She took a deep breath in and slowly let it out as she stood there, making no effort to walk away from this conversation.

"No strings attached?" she asked, chewing her nail nervously.

"Nope. I'm not a strings-attached type person. I'm making it very clear that this is more of a business transaction type thing."

"But why? Why are you doing this?"

I shrugged and shoved a hand through my hair as I gave

that question some thought.

"I don't know. You're attractive and, for the most part, not too crazy. Plus, I know how it feels to be sexually frustrated. I know how to get women off, so I can offer a solution. Easy as that."

"You make it sound like you're some sort of expert," she said with a snort.

"No, not at all. But I understand how bodies work, and I've never had anyone complain in this department."

"Probably because they were all faking it. I can't imagine you came into it with happiness and a positive attitude. You're probably grumpy in bed, too."

"Only one way to find out," I replied, winking as I rocked back on my heels.

Thirteen

Jasmin

Was I seriously considering this?!

Sex—or even just foreplay—with Brody was insane. I didn't even know the guy. But apparently, that wasn't reason enough for my mind to stop imagining him every time I tried to get myself off. The sleeping part was a bit of a surprise as I never would have thought I was capable of that while asleep, but obviously, my body wanted something I wasn't giving it. And I had a sneaking suspicion *that something* was Brody's cock.

"So, what's it going to be? Do you want my help or not?" he asked, smiling smugly.

How the hell was I supposed to answer that? I didn't know how to do a no-strings-attached hook-up, and it felt weird to just jump right in as if this was something normal people did every day.

"How can you be so nonchalant about this?" I questioned, folding my arms over my chest.

"It's easy."

"Yeah, maybe for you. Not so much for girls."

I took another deep breath, this time forcing myself to release it slowly in hopes that it would help calm my nerves. I knew I could just say no and try to go back to sleep, but there was this excitement that was tingling inside of me at the thought of doing something like this. I may never get a chance like this again, and Brody was a good-looking guy, so it wasn't like I was settling by any means. As long as he kept his mouth shut and didn't act like the grumpy ass I'd come to know in such a short time, we'd be just fine.

"How about a massage?" he offered, nodding to the bed. "I won't touch anywhere you don't want me to. But I can at least work on the knots forming across your shoulders. You're making me tense just from looking at you."

"Wow," I sneered, cocking my head to the side. "You're a real charmer, aren't you?"

"Just take your shirt off and lay down." He rolled his eyes and let out a loud huff.

He went into the bathroom and turned on the light while I did as he asked. I still had my bra on, so I reminded myself that this was no different than wearing a bikini. I was showing the same amount of skin and could really use a massage. If he sucked at it, at least I didn't spend hundreds of dollars on it.

A few seconds later, he returned with a bottle of massage oil. I didn't bother to question why he had it, but it felt promising that this might not be so bad after all. My hair was already pulled up onto my head so it was out of his way as I laid my head to the side and closed my eyes.

I felt the oil on my skin as he gently rubbed it in, his strong fingers skillfully moving across my back. There was a light lavender scent that made me feel even more relaxed as he worked his way up to my shoulders, working the knots that had indeed started to form.

There had been so much pressure and stress trying to get stuff set up for Frosty Fest that I hadn't stopped to take the time to do anything about it. I knew that I would end up going for a spa day after the new year, but this just proved how much I needed it now.

"You're so tight," he said softly, squirting more oil before continuing to work my shoulders.

I ignored his words that stirred a fire deep inside my belly. He had offered to take care of that as well, but for now, this was what I was comfortable with.

"If the pressure gets to be too much let me know, and I'll ease up. I really want to work these out for you, though."

"Thank you," I said, already feeling relaxed. "You're better at this than I thought you would be."

"I'm a licensed massage therapist. I used to do this for a living until I decided to focus on welding."

"Wow. I never would have pegged you for a massage therapist."

"I'm into a lot, but pegging is a no for me."

A nervous giggle shot out of me before I could stop it once I realized my words.

"Sorry, I didn't mean—you know—*pegging*…"

"It would be fine if you did. Talking about sex doesn't bother me, and it shouldn't bother you either. You're safe to talk about things openly with me without fear of being judged."

I was about to respond, but before I could, he hit a trigger, and I yelped in pain.

"Yeah, I thought this might be the case," he said more to himself than me. "Do you mind if I position myself above you so I can get a better grip on this?"

"That's fine."

I felt the bed dip as he climbed up and over me, his legs straddling mine. I tried not to think about how amazing it might feel if we were naked and he was slamming into me from behind.

"Do you mind if I remove this?" he asked, pulling on the back of my bra where it clasped. "I don't want to get it gross with the oil I'm putting on your shoulders, and I would like to get in deeper without it being in the way."

"Sure."

His fingers moved lightly over my skin as I felt him undo the clasp before sliding the straps down my arms. He didn't bother taking it all the way off, just enough that my entire back was bare for him.

I closed my eyes and enjoyed his hands as they worked my sore, tired muscles. He shifted his position slightly as he began focusing on my lower back, the stiffness of his erection brushing against my ass in the process.

I swallowed hard and squeezed my legs together to keep from getting turned on.

"If you want to take your sweats off, I'll do full body and work on the spots where you keep getting cramps from those boots you wear."

"You don't have to do that," I answered, knowing that once my pants came off, it would be all over. I would give in and allow this man to do whatever he wanted to me.

"I know I don't have to. I'm offering. I've seen how you walk after taking them off, and you definitely need it."

I sighed heavily, knowing he was right.

"Okay. If you'll close your eyes, I'll turn around so I can get them off."

"If you trust me, I can take them off without you having to roll over."

I nodded and held my breath as I felt his fingers glide over my skin as he pulled them down.

I expected him to start at the top and work his way down to my feet the way other massage therapists did, but instead, he started with my foot and worked his way up. His fingers kneaded the pads of my feet, making me squirm with how good it felt while also hurting at the same time.

He released one foot, then moved to the other before massaging my legs and thighs.

"Do you want me to massage your ass?" he asked, his voice deeper.

"Is that something you typically do in a massage?" I replied, all of my brain cells on a permanent vacation from how relaxed my body was already feeling.

"If they want it, yes. Do you want it?"

Want it? Like, as in his cock? Yeah, I wanted it. I wanted it real bad.

"Want what?" I asked, hoping for clarification. How was I already this distracted?

"Me to massage your ass," he replied with a chuckle. "You've been a real pain in my ass, so I can only imagine I've been one in yours too. I'm happy to alleviate some of that tension for you."

"Well, since you're the one who caused it, go right ahead."

I should have known that him massaging my ass would mean that my panties would have to come off—but again, I wasn't thinking. My body was on fire as he grabbed the top and pulled them down my legs, moving his body along as he did, definitely getting the perfect view of my pussy along the way.

I wanted to cross my legs and hide myself from his view, but the moment he squirted oil on my ass, I was gone. There was nothing left to fight at this point, and it was better just to accept the sweet, delicious torture that was headed my way.

His fingers gripped my ass firmly, then his palms flattened as he used deep strokes, stretching the muscles.

"Oh my God," I whimpered, enjoying the sensation as he relieved tension but also getting super turned on by how close he was getting to my pussy.

"Do you want me to go harder?"

"Yes," I panted. "Harder. Faster. Deeper. Give me all of it."

He chuckled and applied more pressure as he continued massaging my ass. I arched my back, giving him access to where he needed as he applied more oil and started rubbing his way down my cheeks, getting painfully close to my pussy.

"Roll over," he commanded, pulling his hands away while my brain tried to keep up with what he was asking for.

Not caring that I was fully on display anymore, I did as he asked, not bothering to cover my breasts with the bra that was now lying beneath me.

He took his time looking at my body as he rubbed oil between his hands and then leaned forward and began massaging my shoulders from the front. I hated him being so close to where I needed him yet so far away.

"It's okay to let it build," he said softly, looking down at me. "It'll just make your release more intense. And trust me, it'll be worth it."

I nodded and closed my eyes as his hands traveled down over my breasts, gently caressing each as they hung heavily in his grip. I wanted him to lower his mouth and take one of the pebbled nipples into it and suck, but he didn't. He just kept moving down my body until he reached my pussy.

"Shaved. I like it."

He looked up and locked eyes with me, his head hovering where I wanted him, but he didn't move until I nodded my head, confirming this was what I wanted. The next thing I knew, he was fully seated in between my thighs, his tongue sliding along my slit as I gasped and gripped his hair.

"Fuck," I cried out, my body nearly bucking off the bed.

But he didn't seem bothered by it as he pushed my legs down with firm hands and held them in place while he tortured me with his tongue. He nipped at my clit a few times before pulling it into his mouth and sucking. The sensation was driving me mad, nearly sending me over the edge when I was already on the brink.

I could feel the orgasm building as my spine tingled.

"I'm so close," I warned, though it wasn't like he needed it. I could tell he knew by how he changed position and began finger fucking me with two fingers. He was hitting a spot I didn't even know I had while continuing to suck my clit with the right amount of pressure.

"FUCK!" I screamed, panting as waves of pleasure washed over me. My body spasmed so hard that I saw stars again as I felt fluid come out of me.

He pulled away slowly, removing his fingers as he sat beside me on the bed.

I opened my eyes and found him looking at me with a satisfied grin while I avoided looking down to see what kind of mess I made.

"Don't worry about it," he assured me, already reading my thoughts again. "I told you I like it messy. Squirting is fun, isn't it?"

Fourteen
Brody

The sound of snoring kept me up as Jasmin slept comfortably after squirting in my bed. She apologized profusely about the mess, but I assured her it was fine. That was one thing about me—I was rigid with most things in life, but sex wasn't one of them. The messier, the better.

I rolled over, groaning under my breath when I realized I would have to be up in an hour. It would be a long, coffee-fueled day due to the lack of sleep, but thankfully, there wasn't much physical labor that I could do with the second wave of snow that came through last night. The news had assured us we'd seen the worst of it, but given the two feet of fresh snow that had fallen—and continued to fall—I was calling bullshit.

Without waking her up, I rolled out of bed and headed for the shower. There was no point in delaying the inevitable; might as well get up and get the day started. I was still sexually frustrated after last night but declined her offer to get me off. While I had crossed the line with everything I did to her, I was convinced I still had a chance at keeping things from getting too complicated if I stopped it there. The last thing I needed was another complication.

The hot water sprayed down on me, melting away a fraction of the stress sitting on my shoulders. I hated that

I couldn't get outside and work on what I needed to, but there was nothing that could be done about that now. The bigger problem was that Jasmin would be stuck with me even longer now that another storm had rolled in. The chances of her getting out of here and back to Sugarplum Falls safely were slim.

I squirted some shampoo into my hand and lathered it in my hair, closing my eyes as I leaned back into the water. It felt nice, but not as nice as her pussy had felt pressed against my face as I drew her orgasm out of her. Her body was beautiful, and I enjoyed exploring every inch of it.

I finished my shower and got out, drying off quickly so I could free the bathroom in case she needed it. There was another one down the hall, but I knew how much she preferred using this one. I threw on a hoodie and a pair of joggers, then slowly opened the door after turning off the light. She was still sprawled out on my bed, fast asleep.

There was a lot to get done, but unfortunately, the majority of it was outdoor stuff. I would need to check on the reindeer and make sure they had plenty of food and water, but that could wait until the sun was up. It was too cold outside to risk getting stuck out there and freezing to death. I knew they were safe in the barn and had everything they needed until it was safe to venture outside.

I started a pot of coffee and debated on what to make for breakfast. I was too tired to put much effort into cooking, but I also wanted to make sure crazy boot lady had a warm meal to eat. I opened the cabinets and looked around, hoping that something quick and easy would pop out at me. As the coffee started to trickle into the pot, the heavenly aroma filled my senses, giving me hope that today would be a productive day after all.

Settling on a boxed muffin mix, I poured myself a cup of coffee and preheated the oven. The recipe was easy enough, only needing some water, oil, and a few eggs. I added everything to the mixing bowl and then poured the mixture into the large muffin pan that I had already lined. I didn't make muffins often, but when I did, I liked them big instead of those tiny little muffins you had to eat five of just to get full.

I set the pan in the oven and grabbed my cup of coffee as I sat down at the table. It was quiet in the house, which was what I loved the most about it. Being this far outside of town meant there wasn't anyone around to bother me— other than a feisty woman who was obsessed with getting my reindeer.

I opened the book I had been reading and kicked my feet up on the chair across from me, getting comfortable as she walked in.

"Good morning," I said, trying to immediately eliminate any awkward tension after what happened last night. I knew she was self-conscious about a lot, but I didn't want this to be something she regretted.

"Morning." She smiled, but it was as tight as her hair pulled up on top of her head. She padded across the hardwood floor barefoot as she headed to the coffee pot.

"Muffins are baking in the oven and should be ready soon," I offered, keeping my head down and attempting to look like I was reading.

"Thank you. You don't have to keep cooking for me."

"I don't mind."

"Well, since it seems I'm going to be stuck here longer than a few days thanks to the storm outside, I can help cook if you want. Maybe I can fix dinner tonight?"

I lowered my book and folded my hands on top of it as I looked at her.

"I don't know. Are *you* trying to poison me now?"

"Not at all. I wouldn't even know where to begin." She smirked as she poured herself some coffee and then looked at me again. "You like your chicken a little pink, don't you?"

I shook my head, the corners of my lips already starting to curl into a smile from how cute she looked.

"No, Princess," I said as I stood up and walked past her to refill my coffee cup. "It's not *chicken* that I like a little pink. It's that tight little pussy of yours."

I heard a soft gasp escape her lips as her head whipped up to look at me. I winked and finished filling my cup before walking away and letting that image simmer in her head.

Fifteen

Jasmin

"You have got to be kidding me," I groaned into the phone, closing my eyes as I rubbed my fingers against my temple. "How did that happen?"

I waited as Bert went on about how the truck that was supposed to be delivering the Christmas tree for Frosty Fest got stuck on the highway and had to turn around.

"So I'm stuck without a tree for the festival?"

"Sorry, Jasmin. I offered to try to help him get it here, but there's no easy way into Sugarplum Falls. This storm has shut down the roads in and out of town. Even if we brought in extra help to try to get it here, we would just be putting more lives at risk."

"No, you're right. I understand, and I wouldn't want anyone to risk going out in that storm. I'll just have to get creative and see if I can figure something else out."

"Okay. Let me know if I can help. Sam said you might need your driveway cleared soon so I can take the snowplow over and start working on it if you want me to."

"Thank you for the offer, but I'm not at home. I came out to the Truman ranch to discuss securing the reindeer for the event and didn't make it out before the storm happened."

"Isn't Mr. Truman's grandson a real pain in the ass?" Bert asked with a deep chuckle.

"To say the least. But thank you for letting me know about the tree situation. I'll see what I can do and touch base if I need anything."

"Sounds good. Take care, Jasmin."

"You too, Bert."

I hung up the phone and let my head fall back as I chewed the inside of my cheek in frustration. It felt like everything with Frosty Fest was falling apart, and I was trapped out here—in the middle of nowhere—unable to do anything about it.

"Everything okay?" Brody asked, eyeing me as he walked into the kitchen where I was sitting at the table.

"No, but it will be." I sighed heavily, scribbling down a note to find a new tree.

It wasn't that we didn't have other trees to put up in the mall for Frosty Fest. It was that we always had a beautiful, ginormous one in the middle of the mall that everyone loved to look at. Many times, we used it as a giving tree and put up tags for local families who needed a little extra help during the holidays. People would grab a tag and then leave a wrapped present with that person's name on it under it until Frosty Fest. Then, after the parade, Santa and Mrs. Claus would gather around it, handing out the gifts.

"Anything I can help with?" he offered, surprising the shit out of me. Since when did he offer to help with anything? What had happened to his whole, *I'm too busy for you* spiel he had been giving me since the moment I approached him about the reindeer?

"*You* want to help me?" I questioned in disbelief.

He shrugged as if it wasn't a big deal—but it was. Brody had been quick to *help* last night with the whole massage thing, which absolutely had a happy ending. But now he was offering to help me with something related to Frosty Fest? Maybe he was unwell this morning and I shouldn't have had a muffin after all.

"I don't have much else I can do today since the storm hasn't stopped, and I'm bored. So yeah, I want to help. What's going on with the Frozen Palooza?"

"Frosty Fest," I said as nicely as I could through gritted teeth. Why couldn't he just remember the name? It wasn't that hard. But then again, he was still calling me Princess and Crazy Boot Lady, so maybe names weren't his thing.

"Alright, what's going on with *Frosty Fest*?" He rolled his hand for me to get to the point.

I rolled my eyes and shook my head, wishing I had one of Sam's lattes to calm me down right now.

"The company I was using to secure a twelve-foot-tall Douglas-fir for the festival had trouble getting into town due to the storm. They had to turn around, which means we don't have a tree."

"Sugarplum Falls is literally in the middle of the mountains. Why not just cut one down and call it a day?"

"Because you can't do that. You can't just go around town cutting down trees, Brody. There are laws against that."

"Okay, what about a tree farm? Surely you guys have

one of those? I've seen how obsessed the town is with Christmas, so you can't tell me you guys don't have a Christmas tree farm. *That* would be a sin."

"We do," I said, exhaling heavily as I leaned back in the chair. "The problem is that they don't have anything that big. All of their trees are between five to seven feet tall. I need something bigger. I was lucky to snag the twelve-foot one and paid extra to have the guy haul it into town for us. But now he can't make it, and we needed the tree to go up like yesterday."

"But I thought the festival wasn't for a few more weeks?" He pulled his brows together in confusion as he sat down across from me.

"It's not, but we put the big tree up early since it's a giving tree. The festival takes place at the mall, where there's a lot of foot traffic. It encourages people to shop for the people who've left tags on the tree if it's already there and they see it."

He nodded as if it all finally made sense.

"So, the guy who was hauling it in doesn't live in Sugarplum Falls?"

"No. He lives in the next town over. But my friend Bert said all of the roads in and out of Sugarplum Falls are bad. No one can get through. Bert offered to help the guy get it here, but it's too dangerous. He has a big truck and one of the few snowplows in town, but I don't think it's a match for what this storm has brought in."

"Do you think he could get out here?"

"I don't know," I answered with a shrug of my shoulders.

"Possibly. It's only thirty minutes from here to Sugarplum Falls, so he might be able to clear the roads easily. They are somewhat narrow, but who knows? It's a lot shorter of a distance than what he would have to go to help Tim, the guy with the tree."

"Well, if he can get out here and clear the roads, I will get you a tree."

I shook my head, not wanting to believe something good was about to happen.

"I'm sorry—what?"

"Call Bert and see if he can make it out here and clear the roads. If so, I'll help you get a tree to the mall for the Frozen Palooza."

"Frosty Fest," I corrected.

"Same difference."

"It's not, actually." I folded my arms over my chest and arched an eyebrow at him.

"Do you want a tree or not?"

I tipped my head back and exhaled heavily.

"Fine. But only because I literally have no other choice."

"Call him and let me know what he says. I'm going to go check on the reindeer and feed them. I'll be back in soon."

I nodded and grabbed my phone, the call already ringing before Brody could step outside.

Sixteen
Brody

"You guys like it out here, don't you?" I patted the tops of the reindeer's heads and smiled at how well they were doing. My grandfather wasn't lying when he said they enjoyed the cold weather.

I had checked the barn to make sure everything was still secure and that the wind hadn't damaged anything before refilling their food and water bins. They all seemed plenty happy, and being around them reminded me so much of spending time here with my grandfather.

"So, Bert is on his way," crazy boot lady said, startling me as I spun around to find her in the barn with us. Her smile stretched across her face as the reindeer immediately went to her, loving the attention she gave them as she patted their heads and scratched behind their ears.

"Wow. I've never seen them do that before. It's like they know you…"

"I told you we were friends," she replied sarcastically, looking up at me from under her thick lashes.

"Yeah, but what you haven't told me is what are you doing out here?" I asked, hating that she thought it was a good idea to come out in this weather with those stupid boots.

"I came to tell you the good news. And since he is bringing his snowplow, he can free my car while he's here, and I can get out of your hair."

"Let me make myself clearer—why are you coming out in at least two feet of snow with those crazy boots on? Are you trying to break your ankle?"

"No, silly. I borrowed yours. I found an extra pair in the closet, so I slipped them on and came out. I knew you'd be mad if I wore my other boots, so I made an executive decision to steal yours."

"I hate to break it to you, but those aren't mine." I bent down and added the last of the bag of feed to the trough to replenish what they'd already eaten and tossed the empty bag into the vacant stall behind me.

"Oh," she said, frowning as she looked down and lifted her foot. "Whose are they?"

"My grandfather's. And he had pretty bad athlete's foot, so I would be sure to wash your feet really well after you take them off."

Her face fell and I could see her debating on whether to rip them off now or wear them back into the house.

"So, since you're already out here and your friend is on the way, did you want to help pick out the tree?" I offered, wiping my hands on the front of the jeans I changed into before coming outside.

"Sure. That would be nice, thank you."

"Follow me and try not to break anything in the process," I said, looking over my shoulder to see her already struggling to stay upright in the thick snow.

We walked for a few minutes until we got to the edge of the ranch where it was covered with thick forest and plenty of trees to choose from.

"Take your pick," I offered. "Some are well over twelve feet; however, you'll need to make sure Bert is able to get it back. I wouldn't go crazy and do any over fifteen feet."

"No, I think around twelve feet is perfect. We don't want it too big because then it'll be hard to decorate the top. Just something bigger than the other trees we'll have up as decoration throughout the mall."

"Have you guys already gotten those trees?"

"Yeah. Thankfully, one of the tree farms always donates a few to us for Frosty Fest each year. We put little signs up, promoting the farm for them, so it's a win-win."

"Alright. Just let me know which one, and I can get started."

She looked around and then up at me with a confused look.

"Are you just going to demand that it come down?" she asked, folding her arms over her chest as I watched her shiver in the cold.

"No, smart ass. I have tools. They're over in that shed but I didn't want to lug them around until I knew which one I was cutting down."

"You're so grumpy," she said, shaking her head.

"Because you're so difficult."

"I didn't ask you to come out here and cut down a tree for me—you offered."

"Yeah, because I was trying to be nice. Maybe this is a good reminder of why I don't do that anymore."

"You know what—just give me the stupid tools and I'll cut it down myself." She extended her hand as if I were going to give her something that small to cut a giant tree down with. She was certifiably out of her mind.

"The last thing I'm going to do is give you tools. I don't think so."

"And why not?" She placed her hands on her hips and glared at me from beneath the beanie she'd stolen as well.

"Because the last thing I need is you cutting off a limb or something. No thanks."

"Is it because I'm a *woman?* I'll have you know that I am more than capable of a lot of things, Mr. Grumpy Pants, and I don't need your approval for any of them."

"You're right. You don't need my approval for anything. You won't, however, be touching my tools. I don't need you killing yourself out here and leaving me with the mess to deal with."

She huffed out a breath, her chest rising and falling heavily as she cocked her head at me.

"You would like that, wouldn't you? If I died, you wouldn't have to put up with me anymore or deal with me wanting your precious reindeer."

"I literally just said that I don't need any of that right now. What part are you not hearing?"

"You're just trying to make things more difficult because you get off on watching me get angry with you."

"You have no clue what I get off on," I said sternly, stepping into her space so close that I could feel her warm breath on my face as she tipped her head up to look at me.

"In fact, I do. Sandwiches. And doing dirty stuff to them as you make them."

"Don't act like you didn't get all hot and bothered with that as well. *You* were the one who had to run off to go relieve some tension in the bathroom seconds after it happened."

Her jaw dropped open as her dark eyes narrowed at me.

"You have some nerve."

"Yeah, and you're getting on the very last one. Tell me which tree you want so I can send you back inside and cut it down."

"No," she said, with a huff, shaking her head. "I'll tell you which one, but I'm staying out here to watch you cut it down."

"Why? Do you get off on watching me work? Does the thought of me working with an ax turn you on?" I inched closer, lifting her chin with my finger as she tried to look away. "You already know what I can do with my hands and mouth. I bet you're just dying to know what my cock can do."

"Ha," she snarled, pulling away from my touch with such force she almost fell over. "Nothing impressive, I'm sure."

I rubbed my lips together, noticing how she kept trying to avoid looking at me but failed as she watched me out of the corner of her eye.

 "If the size of this tree impresses you, my one-eyed monster is sure to send you over the edge."

Before she could speak, I heard the sound of snow crunching in the distance and took a steady step back.

"I told you she would be out here, likely trying to kill him," the taller man from the coffee shop said, nudging the guy beside him.

"Jasmin isn't going to kill anyone, but my wife might if I don't get home before supper," a burly man with a ballcap on said.

She spun around, nearly losing her balance in the shoes that were at least three sizes too big for her. I was impressed she was able to get as far as she did without falling over in them, but it seemed her luck was coming to an end. I reached my hand out to try to steady her, but it was quickly swatted away as she attempted to walk toward the men approaching us.

"Sam! Aiden! What are you guys doing here? I thought Bert was coming on his own." She reached up and hugged the one I recognized from the coffee shop, not that I could remember his name. I had only been there a few times since I moved to Sugarplum Falls, and it wasn't like I was trying to make friends or get to know anyone.

"We offered to come help with the tree. I know how important it is to you and how you've been so stressed with everything happening with Frosty Fest. We thought if we all came out, we could make sure to get the tree back safely and help clear the road so you guys could get out," the coffee guy said, letting go of her as she wrapped him in a tight hug.

"I'm Sam," he said, reaching past her to extend his hand to me. "I own Sugarplum Lattes."

"Yeah, I recognized you but couldn't remember your name. I'm sorry. Names aren't my thing." I cast a glance at Jasmin, only remembering her name because the other guy said it a few minutes ago.

"No worries. This is Aiden. He owns Sugar Faced Bar—the place to go when the holidays start getting to you," Sam joked with a wink as he clapped Aiden on the shoulder. "And this is Bert. He's got that beast of a snowplow and will work his magic to get you guys out of here."

"Nice to meet you guys," I said, waving my hand, knowing I would forget their names in a minute.

"Most of the road was already cleared up here, so I didn't have to do much. I'll clear the rest of the driveway and the sides of the road so you don't have to worry about snow falling and blocking you in again," Bert said, tugging on his hat.

"Thank you. I appreciate it."

"Cool, so did you have a tree picked out?" Sam asked, rubbing his hands together as he looked at Jasmin.

I hated the feeling that lingered deep in my gut as I watched his eyes light up as he looked at her. I had no idea if she had a boyfriend back home—I guess I should have thought to ask that before everything happened last night. But she was clear in giving her consent and didn't seem to mind as we crossed that line together.

"I think I want that one," she said, pointing to the one behind me. "But *someone* won't let me cut it down."

"That's because *someone* doesn't want to have to deal with you cutting off a limb and taking your ass to the hospital, *Princess*," I replied, matching her snark.

"You guys fight like an old married couple," Sam joked, shaking his head as he grinned. "But he's right, Jas. You're not in any position to try to cut down a tree."

"And why not? I swear to God, if one of you says it's because I'm a woman, I will lose my shit."

"No one ever said it's because *you're a woman*," I answered defiantly, arms over my chest. "I said you can't cut the tree down because you're wearing shoes that are a hazard as well as an oversized coat—that is also a hazard. If you're not wearing the right stuff, I'm not allowing you anywhere near my tools."

"Yeah, well, you've done nothing but complain about my boots since the moment I got here."

"That's because they're better suited for dancing on a stage than trekking around a ranch in the middle of a fucking blizzard."

We were face to face again, both crowding each other's space as the others silently watched around us. I heard a chuckle here and there, which made it hard to stay focused on whatever she was really mad about.

"Are you insinuating that my boots are *stripper* boots?" she exclaimed, eyes wild with anger.

"If the shoe fits…"

"You know what, the shoe is gonna fit. It's gonna fit right up your ass as I take the heel and shove it so far u—"

"That's enough," Sam said, wrapping his arm around her waist and swinging her behind him. "Take her inside and get her stuff together. It won't be long getting this tree down, and then we can head back to town before the roads start freezing."

"Will do," Aiden said, leading Jasmin back to the house as she glared at me over her shoulder.

I scrubbed a hand over my face, trying to get rid of the frustration she had caused.

"Man, I know that look when I see it," Sam said, shaking his head.

"What look?"

"The look of a man who is trying desperately not to fall for the woman who is driving him crazy. If you want to hang in town for a bit tonight, Aiden makes a drink called Dirty Reindeer Balls that will fix that and all of your problems."

I lifted my eyebrows in worry as he laughed.

"I don't know about that," I said. "But I do know that if we don't get this tree down soon, we're going to lose daylight, and no one will be going anywhere."

"Let's get it done," Sam replied, following me to the shed with Bert right behind us.

Seventeen

Jasmin

I sang Christmas carols at the top of my lungs the entire way from the ranch to Sugarplum Falls and didn't even mind that we were going fifteen miles an hour the majority of the time. While the guys were able to clear the roads, there were still layers of ice that we had to be careful of.

Bert led the way with his snowplow, deviating every now and then to clear more of the road when he could. Sam and Aiden were piled in his truck with him, which left Brody following in his truck behind me. He had the tree secured, which I was incredibly grateful for. But not as grateful as I was to be by myself and away from him for a bit.

Brody had his good moments—though they were few and far between. I didn't know how I was going to spend another day cooped up with Mr. Grumpy Ass. He didn't even have a single Christmas decoration up in his house, and when I asked him about it this morning, he seemed confused as to why I would think he would decorate. *Hello, it's Christmas!*

We needed a break from each other—that was for sure. I still hadn't solved the reindeer crisis, but at least I had the tree fiasco taken care of. I had already spoken with Andi, who had rallied a team together at the last minute to meet at the mall and help us get it decorated. She had her staff handing out the giving tree cards for those who wanted to fill them out. Anyone could take their tag and hang it on the tree when they wanted to, as long as it was up a few days before Frosty Fest so people had a chance to shop.

I grinned when Sugarplum Falls finally came into view and debated on heading directly to Sugarplum Lattes. I could get in and out before anyone would miss me and could really use a latte right now. As if reading my mind, Bert pulled to the side of me and rolled down his window. I rolled mine down and frowned when I saw Sam lean forward.

"We closed early so I could have everyone help out with decorating the tree."

My face fell with disappointment as I nodded my head and rolled the window back up. I got back in line behind them and followed them to the mall, parking in my assigned space.

I left the guys to get the tree situated after they assured me for the hundredth time that they didn't need my help. I went to my office, set my stuff down, and checked the handful of notes that had been left on my desk. It was all stuff I was aware of, thankfully, and no new fires had started while I was gone.

By the time I finished, the tree was already inside, and a handful of people were helping to set it up. Thankfully, this was relatively easy, given how many years we'd been doing it. Everyone knew what needed to be done.

"It's beautiful," Andi said, standing beside me as we watched them get it secured.

"It is, isn't it?"

"So much bigger than I thought it would be." She tilted her head back to take it all in.

"Yeah, the original one I was trying to get was twelve feet. Brody let me pick which one I wanted from the ranch, and this one just called to me. I think the guys said it's almost fourteen feet. It's going to be a pain in the ass to try to decorate the top, but I think we can figure it out."

"Hey, Jasmin?" Cody said nervously, looking at me with a scrunched face.

"What's up, Cody?" I asked, giving him as much of my attention as I could as I watched the guys step back from the tree. I think everyone was afraid it might be too big and too heavy for the base we had, but thankfully, it didn't sway or move an inch once they let go.

"I have some bad news."

I turned to face him, my heart already sinking from the look on his face. Nothing good came from the look of devastation on a teenager's face.

"What is it? What's wrong?"

I felt Brody's presence but ignored it as I waited for Cody to spit it out.

"Ummm. You know the sign that we use every year for Santa and Mrs. Claus?"

"Yeah…"

"Well… It umm… It broke."

"What?!" I exclaimed, my hand flying to my chest. "What do you mean *it broke*? How bad is it? Can we fix it?"

"I don't think so. I'm sorry. The new kid was getting the boxes of decorations down in the storage room, and he didn't see it up there. It fell to the floor and shattered. We cleaned up the glass and tried to save the strand of lights, but those broke too."

I slowly inhaled, closing my eyes as I processed the news.

"I'm so sorry. We didn't mean for it to happen. He had no idea it was up there, and I should have thought to tell him about it beforehand."

"It's okay, Cody. Accidents happen. Thank you for telling me. I'll figure something out."

He lowered his head and nodded as he walked away.

"What kind of sign?" Brody asked, still standing right beside me.

I opened one eye and glared at him. We weren't stuck together at the ranch anymore, so he didn't need to be in my space.

"It's a light-up sign that says Santa and Mrs. Claus. One of the Frosty Fest founders made it, and we've used it every year since the festival began. We always set up a bench beside the giving tree and then hang the sign above the bench. Santa and Mrs. Claus sit there to hand out the presents that were collected to those who participated."

"I know it sucks, but we can still set up the bench without the sign," Aiden offered, lifting his brows sympathetically at me.

"I mean, I guess we'll have to," I said with a heavy sigh, rubbing a finger against my temple.

"Woah, what's wrong?" Sam asked, joining us and looking around as he handed me a cup of coffee.

My eyes widened when I saw my name on the side.

"The Claus sign broke," Andi explained, taking the other cup from him that had her name on it.

"You brought me coffee?" I asked in disbelief.

"Well, technically, I had Jeremy make you coffee. He brought the orders over after he closed up, so they should still be hot."

"Thank you, that's so sweet. You have no idea how badly I've been craving a gingerbread latte," I replied with a soft laugh.

"Trust me. I know. I told Jeremy not to forget the extra whipped cream as well."

I glanced up to find Brody standing there with his arms folded over his chest and brows furrowed.

"You know her drink order?" he asked Sam, a new level of assertiveness laced in his deep voice.

"I do." Sam nodded, lifting a cup to his lips as Jeremy came over, carrying two more to-go trays filled with drinks. "I know everyone's orders. It's my gift."

They stared each other down and I couldn't help but wonder who might win if they ended up in a brawl. I initially thought Sam could kick Brody's ass, but seeing them next to each other, I wasn't so sure. Both were about the same height and build, but Brody had defined muscles in places I hadn't noticed on Sam.

"Interesting," Brody muttered, looking away before Sam pulled a cup from the tray and handed it to him.

"Salted caramel cold brew. I know you said you don't care for sweet drinks, but I noticed the way your face changed when you had a sip, so I thought it was a safe bet."

"You remembered what I ordered?" Brody questioned in disbelief. "I went there *once* while you were working. Some other guy helped me the other time I went in."

"I'm always there and know what's happening. Trust me, I know what you ordered."

"Well, thank you." Brody lifted his drink and took a sip.

"Alright, now that we all have caffeine, thanks to Sam and Sugarplum Lattes, let's get this tree decorated," I announced, lifting my cup in the air as we all cheered Sam and his crew for the drinks.

Everyone scattered about, knowing who would handle what. The guys worked on getting the ladders to begin stringing the lights around the monstrous beast of a tree while the rest of us began sorting through the different bins of ornaments.

"What's the theme this year?" Andi asked, holding up a red glittery round ornament in one hand and a white snowflake in the other.

"I think, since we've had such a wild winter already, we go with *Cold as Ice*. All white decorations which will go well with the white lights. I can work on getting some white lanterns that we can float throughout the mall to help pull things together as well."

"Sounds perfect. I'll get everyone started on picking white decorations, and then we'll put the rest back in storage."

I smiled at Andi, loving how helpful she was.

I pulled out my phone and made a few notes to look for more white decorations to pull everything together. As I tucked it back into my pocket, I looked up to find Brody headed my way.

"Hey, do you have some extension cords?" he asked.

It felt odd to see him stick around and help out when he could have easily said *see ya* after getting the tree unloaded. He had made it clear that he had no intentions of making friends, so why was he still here?

"Yeah, they're in my office. I'll go grab them."

I turned and headed there, only to find him falling in step beside me.

"You can wait here, and I'll bring them to you," I snapped, hating how much he was getting under my skin again.

"That's alright. I don't mind coming with you."

"Maybe *I* mind."

He just smirked and kept walking as if my words meant nothing to him.

I opened the door, not bothering to make sure it stayed open for him as I stepped inside. It wasn't a huge office, and this time of year, it felt even smaller with all of the stuff

I had crammed in here for the Frosty Fest. I shoved a few boxes out of the way and opened the closet door to grab the extension cords.

"Here you go," I said, shoving a handful at him. "Whatever you don't need, you can just leave them on the floor, and I'll put them away later."

"What's the deal with you and Sam?" he blurted out, catching me by surprise.

"Excuse me?" My brows pulled tightly together.

"You and Sam. What's the deal."

"How is that any of your business?"

"It's not. But I'm still asking."

"Yeah, and I'm refusing to answer." I planted my hands on my hips and glared at him.

"Don't do that."

"Do what?" I threw my hands in the air, confused yet again.

"Put your hands on your hips and glare at me."

My eyes narrowed so far that I could barely see out of the slits as I placed my hands back on my hips and stepped toward him.

"I will do whatever the hell I want, and nothing you say or do is going to stop me. Do you underst—"

Before I could get my words out, Brody's arm locked behind my waist, pulling me flush against his chest as his lips lowered to mine. The kiss wasn't gentle but filled with hunger as his mouth desperately fought to claim mine.

I immediately tried to pull away, but then his hand slipped down to my ass and gripped it so hard that I froze as his other hand firmly held the back of my neck, keeping me in place. My lips parted, accepting him in as my fingers quickly began tugging at strands of his hair while I tried to get more of him.

Just as things were really heating up, he stepped away and broke the kiss. His hazel eyes frantically searched for something on my face while I attempted to catch my breath. That was by far the *hottest* kiss I'd ever had.

"I'm going to ask one more time," he said sternly, rubbing his fingers across his jawline. "What's the deal with you and Sam?"

"Nothing," I immediately answered. "Sam is a really good friend. Nothing more than that."

"Are you sure? He knew your drink order."

"Sam knows everyone's drink order," I countered breathlessly. "You could go out and quiz him right now and he would be able to tell you every single person's order."

He nodded as if this information satisfied him, then grabbed the extension cords he'd thrown on the chair and left.

What in the world just happened? Was Brody seriously jealous of Sam?

Eighteen
Brody

It was way later than I expected when I finally finished helping with the tree and wanted to leave. The sun had already set hours ago, bringing with it a drastic drop in temperature. I shivered as I climbed into my truck and turned the key in the ignition, frustrated when it wouldn't start.

I tried again and again, not ready to admit defeat. Finally, I got out and headed back into the mall to see where the nearest automotive shop was. I knew my grandpa's truck was old and needed quite a few repairs, but those had been on my to-do list as well.

Just as I was heading in, I spotted Aiden and Sam coming out. I tried to ignore the jealousy I felt every time Sam interacted with Jasmin, but I believed her when she said nothing was going on between them. Throughout the day, he had been the same with everyone—male and female—which helped reassure me that he didn't have the hots for the girl I'd just made out with in her office.

"Forget something?" Sam asked, both of them stopping to talk with me.

I shoved a hand through my hair and looked over at my truck as Bert came out. I still felt a bit of jealousy toward him but had time to process it and realized that it wasn't that Sam was coming onto Jasmin. I was jealous of how *she* reacted to him.

"I was going to see if someone could point me in the direction of the nearest automotive shop. I think the battery died."

"The closest shop closed an hour ago," Bert replied. "And I know your grandfather mentioned that the alternator was having some issues as well."

"Lovely," I muttered, trying not to sound like a dick. I just wanted to get home and call it a day. "Would someone mind giving me a jump to see if that works until I can get back tomorrow to deal with stuff?"

"Sure. I'm parked around back, but I'll meet you at your truck in a few," Aiden offered, rushing off to go get it.

"I hate to be the bearer of bad news, but I don't think you're getting home tonight," Sam said softly as they joined me at my truck.

"Yeah, I hate to admit it, but I think you might be right. I'll check and see if I can get a room somewhere for the night."

"Everything is sold out," Bert said, rubbing a hand across his round stomach. "That storm stranded a lot of people trying to pass through, so everything filled up quickly. I have a cabin that I would offer, but I already lent it to this friendly couple that couldn't get a room either."

I didn't like the sound of where this was going.

Aiden pulled up and we got busy trying to jump-start the truck. Just as expected, nothing worked.

"Hey, what's going on?" Jasmin asked, walking past us

with her coat pulled tight and bags full of stuff layered on both arms.

"His battery died," Sam said. "He's stuck here for the night."

"Oh. Is someone going to give him a ride to a hotel?" she asked, looking between the guys.

"Everything is full," Bert said. "I would offer to take him in, but my in-laws are already staying with us, so we don't have the space."

"It's not a big deal. I can sleep in the truck," I offered, ready to be done with all of this.

"You can't sleep in the truck," Jasmin replied, looking at me as if I were an idiot.

"I don't see any other options here. I can't get home, and everything in town is booked."

"I know exactly where he can go," Sam said with a mischievous smile.

We all stared at him, waiting for the big reveal.

"Jas has a spare room and could use some help with the decorations she's taking home. Seems like a win-win to me."

Jasmin's eyes bulged as her jaw dropped.

"I… No… That's not… No." She shook her head defiantly.

"Come on, Jas," Sam said, stepping closer to her and taking some of the bags from her arms. "He helped you when you had nowhere to go. You can repay the favor. Besides, it's only for one night until he can get his truck fixed tomorrow."

She continued to stare at him as she thought about it before closing her eyes and exhaling heavily.

"Fine. Mr. Grumpy Ass can stay with me. But it's freezing out here, so hurry up. I'm not waiting all night for you."

Sam caught my eye as he handed me the bags he'd taken from her, then clapped me on the back.

"Have fun," he said, winking before climbing into Aiden's truck and shutting the door.

This was definitely a turn of events I didn't see coming.

Nineteen

Jasmin

"Your steering wheel is going to fall off if you grip it any tighter," Brody said, nodding to my death grip.

"That's for me to worry about."

"I beg to differ. If you rip the steering wheel off, the car crashes and we both could get hurt. Or worse, die."

"Yeah, well, sometimes sacrifices have to be made."

I didn't bother to look at him as he chuckled in the passenger seat beside me. I pulled into the driveway and waited for the garage door to open before pulling in and parking. Brody didn't ask before he opened the other back door and began helping me take in all the stuff I'd brought home to work on for Frosty Fest.

I held the garage door open with my hip while allowing him to go past me since he had his arms full of boxes that were likely blocking his view.

"There's an island in front of you. You can set everything there," I said, flicking the light switch on so he could find it easily.

I set down the bags I was holding and shook my arms, trying to get the feeling back in them.

"It's only one night, but we may as well get the whole house tour thing over and done with," I said, nodding for him to follow me. "This is obviously the kitchen and living room. That hallway leads to the bedrooms and bathrooms, and that way is the front door. You're welcome to head that way at your earliest convenience."

He chuckled under his breath and followed me down the hallway.

"This is the guest bedroom where you'll be staying. There are extra linens in the closet. The guest bathroom is across the hall. I don't have any manly stuff, but you're welcome to help yourself to whatever you need. Extra toothbrushes and soap are in the cabinet."

"What's down there?" he asked, pointing to the other doors that were closed.

"One is my office and the other my bedroom. Both are off limits."

I turned and walked off, not giving him the opportunity to ask any more questions.

"I have a lot of work to catch up on, so I'm not making dinner. I'll order pizza, but if you want something else, you can order your own food."

"Pizza works for me. And I'll pay since I'm crashing here tonight."

"I don't need you to pay for my pizza."

He was in my space again, so close I could smell the faint scent of his soap.

"I never said you *needed* me to do anything. I said I

would pay for dinner. It's my way of saying thank you for allowing me to stay here."

"Oh, so you do have manners. They're not as frequent as they should be, but it definitely seems like we're making progress." I cocked my head to the side and planted my hands on my hips.

"I told you to stop doing that," he warned, pointing to my hands.

"And I told you to stop telling me what to do. You're not the boss of me."

"Don't push me, Jasmin."

I covered my mouth as I gasped dramatically.

"Oh my God! You *do* know my name!"

"Yeah, it's better than calling you Crazy Boot Lady."

My eyes widened as I stared at him.

"*That's* what you've been calling me?"

"Not to your face, *Princess*."

"You know what, maybe I've changed my mind about letting you stay here."

"That's fine. I'll go sleep in my truck. But you're the one who is going to have to live with the thought that they allowed someone to freeze to death in their truck because you were a bit cranky." He rocked back on his heels and smirked at me.

"Ugh. You're the worst. And if anyone is cranky—it's you."

"Actually, I've been in a good mood the past few days. So not so much anymore."

I rolled my eyes and walked back to the living room, ignoring him. I needed to pretend he wasn't here, in my space. I turned on the TV, went straight to my Spotify account, and put on some Christmas music. Then I opened the app on my phone and ordered two large pizzas. A plain pepperoni pizza and meat lovers seemed like good choices since I had no idea what he liked but wasn't willing to ask him.

While waiting for the food to come, I started grabbing the bags from the island and carried them over to the floor in front of the couch. I'd already pushed the coffee table off to the side so it wasn't in the way since I would need a lot of room to work.

"What do you need help with?" Brody asked, staring down at me with his arms folded.

"Nothing. I've got it, but thank you. The food should be here in thirty to forty-five minutes."

"I have nothing else to do, and it looks like you need as much help as you can get. So why don't you stop being so stubborn and just let me help you."

"Fine. Since you won't seem to take *no* for an answer, you can help me put together the raffle baskets."

"Raffle baskets?" he questioned as he sat on the floor beside me.

"Yes, *raffle baskets*," I repeated in a mocking tone. "Local companies donate items for a basket and then we set them up at the mall in display cases with attached boxes for people to bid on them. All of the money raised goes to a different cause each year. Last year, the money went to the local schools to upgrade the playground equipment and to purchase new computers for the high school. The year before that, the funds went to the animal shelter. They were able to do some repairs and expand the facility."

"Wow. That's really cool."

I felt my cheeks heat as I blushed at his genuine compliment. Maybe being stuck together again wouldn't be such a bad thing after all.

124

Twenty
Brody

"Do you have more ribbon?" I asked, lifting the box I was holding and looking beneath it.

"I think we're out, but I can grab more at the store tomorrow." She looked around the floor, moving baskets out of the way.

I didn't want to tell her that she had a bow stuck to her head—mainly because it was so adorable I wanted to enjoy looking at it a little longer.

"Nope. We're out." She sighed heavily and leaned back against the couch as we stared at the pile of gift baskets scattered between us on the floor. We had both devoured the pizzas when they came, and I found myself indulging in a glass of sweet wine afterward. She had calmed down and didn't seem as hostile toward me anymore, which was welcoming. I hated to intrude, but it seemed fate had other plans for us tonight.

"Other than the ribbon for this one, I think we're done," I said, setting the basket down beside the others.

She nodded and looked around.

"Thank you again for your help, Brody. I wouldn't even be done with half of these if I had worked on them by myself.

I appreciate it."

"Not a problem. It's the least I could do for you letting me stay here tonight."

She smiled, and I felt my heart flutter when I noticed how this one reached her eyes. It was like she was genuinely happy with me.

"What else did you need to work on?" I asked, ready to jump into the next project. Normally, this would have felt like work. But *working* with Jasmin didn't feel like work at all. It felt nice, and I hated that it was something I might want to get used to in the future.

"That's all I have for Frosty Fest tonight. The rest of the stuff is still in my office, which I'll bring home tomorrow night to work on. It never ends."

"Do you get a break at all during this whole Frosty Fest thing?"

She shook her head but didn't look sad.

"No. Things stay pretty busy for me from Thanksgiving until the festival is over. There's a lot of planning that goes into the event each year, and then the actual execution to make it all happen. But it's the best time of year, and our town loves it. That's what makes it all worth it."

"You really love Christmas, don't you?"

She smiled again, this one brighter than before. Holy shit, I needed to stop looking at her when she did. It was like I really was a grinch, and each smile she offered helped to make my ice-cold heart grow a size or two bigger. Okay, so maybe it wasn't just my *heart*.

"I do." She nodded happily. "Not that you can tell since I haven't had a chance to decorate here yet. But that's on my list for this weekend. I don't want people to start talking about me because I'm one of the last houses to put my lights up." She laughed, but I knew there was some truth to what she was saying. I hadn't been in town long, but I could already tell how serious the people of Sugarplum Falls took Christmas.

"They really do that?"

"They sure do. Especially the older ladies in town who have nothing better to do than gossip. It's always a hot topic this time of year, and most of us try to get ahead of it by decorating as early as possible to avoid being in the gossip mill."

"Wow. I'm glad I don't have to worry about that," I admitted, running a hand through my hair. "I can't see my closest neighbors, so I doubt anyone would care if I didn't decorate."

"Don't you care though?"

I shrugged, not sure how much of this to get into.

"Not really. I don't really care for the holiday in general, so I see no point in decorating and making a big deal of it. Especially since I live by myself and don't have anyone who comes to visit—aside from pretty girls who get themselves stuck to my fence post while trying to steal my reindeer." I pointed a finger at her as her cheeks flushed red with embarrassment.

"Can I ask you a question?" She tucked her legs beneath her and leaned her side against the couch.

"Sure."

"Why don't you like Christmas?"

I pushed back against the couch I was leaning on and straightened my legs in front of me. This was a hard question, one that I didn't like answering.

"It's just never been my thing."

I was hoping she would leave it at that, but then I remembered how determined she was to talk to me about the reindeer, so I knew she wouldn't.

"Not even as a child?"

My jaw flexed immediately in response. Her eyes widened slightly as she noticed it, but she didn't rush me to answer.

"I used to love Christmas when I was a kid. My dad and I always went to the mountains and cut down our Christmas tree. Then we'd go home and decorate it together. My mom was usually uninterested, so she never bothered to participate. But I didn't mind. My dad and I were incredibly close. He was my best friend."

I could feel her watching me, waiting for me to say the words that would break her heart the same way they did mine all those years ago.

"When I was thirteen, I was waiting for my dad to come home from work so we could pack up and head to the mountains. I had spent the day decorating the house and was so proud of it. I couldn't wait for him to see it. But then he called and said he was going to be late because he got a call to pick my mom up from work. Apparently, she had been drinking on the job and hiding it, only that day, she hit the bottle a little too hard. On their way home, another driver ran a red light and plowed into my parent's car. My dad died immediately, and my mom was taken to the hospital."

"Oh my gosh," she whispered, covering her mouth with her hands as her eyes welled up with tears. "I'm so sorry, Brody."

I nodded, my jaw too tight to try to smile.

"If she hadn't been drunk at the store, my dad would have never had to go out of his way to get her. The accident wouldn't have happened, and he would still be here. But because of her, he died. I know it's terrible to say it, but there's not a day that has gone by that I don't blame her for his death. I know she was struggling and needed help, but I can't forgive her for what she did. She took something from me that I can never get back."

I balled my hands into fists at my side, hating the emotions running through me after admitting that out loud.

"Because of her, I lost my best friend one week before Christmas. She took everything away from me with her addiction."

A hot tear ran down my cheek, and before I knew it, Jasmin was beside me, pulling me into her arms as I cried for the first time in twenty years.

"I never celebrated Christmas after that. My mom stayed drunk, so she never even noticed it was that time of year and probably relished the fact that she didn't have to do anything for it. No gifts to buy. No Christmas dinner to cook. All of that died the day my dad died. I know that she loved him, and I'm sure that she started to drink more to help her deal with his loss. But it only caused me to lose another parent. She never bothered trying to be there for me or to keep us together as a family."

"I'm so sorry," Jasmin said, her voice breaking as I felt her tears join mine. "That's not fair to you at all. My heart hurts for you and everything you've lost."

"Thank you. I think the hardest part was when she took the baseball and glove set my dad had bought me for Christmas and sold it so she could buy more alcohol. That was the last gift he had given me, and we never even got to use it."

"That's so sad. I couldn't even imagine the pain you must have felt from that."

I nodded, pulling her tighter against me as I allowed her to comfort me in a way no one had before.

Twenty-One

Jasmin

Brody's story broke my heart.

Seeing him break down as he told the story about his father and losing him when he was just a teenager made me understand why he hated Christmas so much. I felt bad for asking, but I also felt honored to know something about him that no one else really knew. It also explained why he didn't have a relationship with his mother, even though it made me angry that she had the nerve to call *him* a grinch. I didn't know her very well and was thankful for that. She definitely didn't sound like someone I wanted to know.

We moved all of the raffle baskets to the kitchen island so they were out of the way. It was incredible how much we had gotten done, and I felt the weight on my shoulders lift. This put me ahead on some of the stuff I had fallen so quickly behind on while I was stuck at Brody's.

"I think I'm going to call it a night," I said to Brody as we cleaned up the last of the supplies we had used for the baskets. "You're welcome to stay up and watch TV or something if you'd like to. Help yourself to anything in the fridge or pantry. Coffee is already set to start brewing in the morning."

"Thank you. I'll probably call it a night as well."

"Well, if you need anything, just let me know."

He nodded his head, but not before I saw the look in his eyes.

Neither of us had bothered to discuss the kiss we'd shared in my office earlier, but I wasn't sure now was the time for it. We were both tired and now emotionally drained after talking about his dad. Not knowing what to do, I leaned in and gave him a quick pat on his pec.

His eyebrow rose as he studied me, but I was too stunned by my own awkwardness to process that I should remove my hand from his body.

"I'm sorry," I said with a nervous laugh. "I don't know what that is. Pretend I didn't just do that."

As I went to pull my hand away, he captured it with his and held it in place before wrapping his other around my waist and pulling me into him.

"I don't regret kissing you earlier, and I'm not going to regret it now, either," he said, his voice low and sultry.

My eyes blinked rapidly as my heart raced in my chest.

While we had already technically been intimate with each other—or more so, him pleasuring me—this felt different. More intimate. There was a connection between us that hadn't been there before. Or if it was, it hadn't felt *this* strong.

He let go of my hand and used his fingers to lift my chin, forcing me to look up at him. Then his lips slowly trailed over mine, the wetness of his tongue coating them.

I parted my lips, allowing him access as his tongue eagerly

began to explore my mouth. His grip on me tightened as if he were afraid to let go. But I wasn't going anywhere. No matter how many times I tried to deny it, this was what I wanted.

I lifted my hands and tugged on his short locks of hair, trying to pull him closer to me. His hands moved down to my ass and gripped it, lifting me to his hips as our mouths continued to try to devour each other.

"My bedroom," I panted, barely pulling my mouth away from his long enough to get the words out.

"I thought you said it was off limits," he teased, carrying me down the hallway.

"I was stupid. It's definitely on limits."

"I don't think that's a thing."

"Ugh. Just shut up and keep kissing me." I grabbed his head in my hands and held it still as I kissed him, thankful I didn't make him trip and fall since he couldn't see where he was going. But Brody struck me as the kind of person who could find his way in complete darkness because within a few minutes, we were in my room and he was lowering me to the bed.

"Clothes off," I insisted, pointing to his hoodie and jeans as I lifted my shirt over my head and tossed it to the floor. He was moving way too slowly for my liking as he watched me shimmy out of my yoga pants and toss them as well. "Now, Brody."

He chuckled and kicked off his boots, painfully slow I might add. Then took his sweet time removing the rest of his clothes, leaving just his black boxer briefs that outlined his erection perfectly.

I swallowed hard as I stared down at it, knowing things were about to get really good.

"Is this what you wanted?" he asked, extending his hands out to his side.

"No." I shook my head. "That's what I want." I pointed to his dick, smiling when he looked down and gripped it with his hand.

"You sure about that?"

"More sure than anything I've ever been surer about before." I knew my words didn't make sense, and I wasn't even sure what order they came out in. None of that mattered because I had cock on the brain, and it was making me stupid. "Now, gimme."

His grin spread across his cheeks as he climbed onto the bed beside me, taking in the matching black lace bra and panty set I had put on earlier when I changed into comfy clothes—not that this was premeditated or anything…

"This is nice," he said, hooking his finger under the thin bra strap and pulling it down before kissing my shoulder.

"Thanks." I closed my eyes and enjoyed the feeling of his tongue on my skin while his hands explored the rest of my body.

"Maybe we should take it off."

"I think that's a great idea. These too," I said, slipping my fingers under the waistband of his boxer briefs.

"Would that make you happy?" he asked, leaning onto his

elbow and watching me.

"Very." I nodded, my eyes lowering as he pulled them off and threw them to the floor. His cock wasn't just long— it was thick and veiny—just how I imagined. I quickly removed my bra and panties, not minding the chill against my skin as a wave of goosebumps spread over it.

I licked my lips and leaned forward, pushing him on his back before lowering myself between his legs.

"Nope," he said, grabbing my thigh and keeping me from moving any further.

"What's wrong? You don't like head?"

"I love it. But I'm not going to wait for my dessert while you get to have yours. Bring that tight little pussy up here, and let me eat it while you're doing that."

My eyebrows shot up in surprise. I had read about people doing this, but I'd never personally tried this position.

"You want to sixty-nine?" I asked, my voice suddenly quiet and uncertain.

"Yeah. It'll be fun. We can get each other off at the same time, then get to the even better stuff."

I chewed my lower lip as I considered it.

"I've never done it before," I admitted.

"We don't have to if you don't want to," he quickly assured me. "I just thought it might be fun. Plus, I really don't want to wait to taste you."

"Okay," I said, nodding my head. "We can try it. How do

you want me to get up there?"

He laid down on his back and then extended his hands to me.

"Climb up here and turn to face the wall, like you would if you were doing reverse cowgirl."

I furrowed my brow, obviously not as experienced in the bedroom as he was.

"Here, give me your hands, and I'll help you."

I did as he said and tried to hold my balance as he guided me until I was practically sitting on his face. My stomach felt like it was on fire as anxiety rushed through me about having my private parts literally in his face. I knew that it wasn't any different with how close they were when he went down on me, but that was different. He could move away at a moment's notice if he didn't want to be down there. In this position, he would be stuck until I decided to move. What if I smothered him? Even worse—what if I accidentally farted or something? No one—and I repeat, NO ONE would be able to come back from that.

"Stop overthinking it," he said, giving my ass a quick slap and freeing me from my obsessive thoughts. "Just sit on my face and stop worrying. I'll be fine. I know how to breathe, and if I die, at least I'll go out doing something I love."

"That's not funny," I said, looking at him over my shoulder. "I don't want to have to tell people that I killed you by sitting on your face."

"You're not going to. I was just kidding."

I scrunched my face and looked away, nearly forgetting all

my worries as I found his cock waiting for me.

I shifted my weight and lowered my head over his dick, slowly taking it into my mouth as I gripped the base of it firmly in my hands. He groaned before covering my slit with his mouth, his tongue quickly parting my folds and swiping in between.

Neither of us was going to last long at this rate, but that didn't matter right now. We had all night to enjoy each other.

My cheeks hollowed as I took him to the back of my throat, knowing he was trying not to come as he squeezed my thighs harder. He began sucking my clit, nearly sending me over the edge as I gagged and worked him harder with my hands, taking a few seconds to caress his balls.

"I don't want to come in your mouth," he said abruptly, pulling away long enough that my clit throbbed from being so close to release.

"Then you'd better fuck me," I replied after pulling him free and stroking him.

I climbed down carefully, making sure not to kick him accidentally. Since he was already on his back, I climbed over and straddled him, sliding him right inside of me.

My eyes closed as I felt his hands on my hips, slowing my motions until I adjusted to him being inside of me. I let my head fall back as my hands roamed over my breasts, the tight buds already begging to be sucked. He lifted his hips and thrust to let me know he was ready.

I opened my eyes and smiled down at him as I leaned forward, allowing my breasts to hang in front of his face.

He eagerly took the lead and began playing with them, pulling each nipple into his mouth and sucking while I rode his cock.

I wanted nothing more than to come, and the way my clit was rubbing against his cock, I could get there very quickly. He sucked harder as if knowing I was already almost there. The combination of pain and pleasure was too much, and within seconds, I felt the walls of my pussy contract and spasm around him as I came.

"Fuck," he growled, pulling away from my breasts as he gripped my hips so hard his fingers dug into my skin. "Shit, Crazy Boot Lady!"

I held back a laugh until I felt his body relax beneath me, knowing that he had come. He sighed heavily, his eyes still shut for a moment while I stared down at him.

When he finally opened them, I playfully narrowed mine at him and put my hands on my hips.

"Did you seriously just yell out *Crazy Boot Lady* as you came?"

Twenty-Two

Brody

"Not only did I call you Crazy Boot Lady, we totally forgot to use protection," I answered with a heavy sigh, brushing a strand of hair out of her face as she lay beside me.

"I'm so sorry! I got lost in the moment and didn't even think about it." She chewed her nails nervously as she looked up at me. "But, if it makes you feel any better, I'm on birth control, and I just got checked at my annual check-up. Nothing to report other than a clean bill of health."

"Before you, I hadn't had sex in at least nine months. I've had a physical done since then and have nothing to report either."

"Well, I'm glad that's settled, but let's get back to the Crazy Boot Lady thing," she said, playfully poking me in the chest.

I grabbed her hand and pulled it across my body, tucking her in closer to my side.

"What?" I shrugged my shoulders. "I couldn't remember your name and all I could think of was those crazy boots you were out trotting around in the snow in."

"I do not *trot*," she corrected. "You make me sound like a turkey or something."

"Well, in that case, let's call it Thanksgiving. I'm ready for a feast." I wiggled my eyebrows and attempted to slide down her body to get between her legs as she laughed and swatted at me.

"As fun as that sounds," she said behind a yawn covered by her hand. "I don't think I could stay awake if I tried. I got dicked good and hard, so now it's time for sleep."

"Since you're laying on my arm and half of my naked body, does that mean I get to stay in your bed tonight? Or am I being banished back to the guestroom down the hall?"

"You can stay, but no funny business. I have a lot to do tomorrow and need all the rest I can get."

"Nope, no funny business at all," I agreed, feeling a weird sensation in my chest as I pulled the blankets up and covered her as she softly snored against me.

****

The next morning, I was pleasantly surprised when Jasmin suggested we shower together. She insisted that it was more time efficient and that we would save water, but I knew deep down she just wanted to see my dick in the broad daylight. I made sure to take my time cleaning up, stroking it from tip to base as she watched.

I was even more surprised when she got dressed for work and put on a pair of jeans, a T-shirt, and tennis shoes. Gone were the crazy boots she wore that always worried me she would break an ankle in. But I had to admit; I liked this look on her as much as I enjoyed her wearing the tight leggings and low-cut tops.

She offered to take me by the automotive shop before

heading to the mall, but I distracted her by asking to stop at Sugarplum Lattes first. It wasn't that I didn't want to fix whatever was wrong with my truck and get back to the ranch. It was that I didn't want to go back without her. I found myself already falling for her in a way I never imagined was possible.

"Are you sure you want to do this?" Jasmin asked as we carried armfuls of baskets into the mall after stopping by her office to drop off our coffee cups and the box of stuff she hadn't gotten to last night.

"For the last time, yes. It'll go faster with two people working on it, so just tell me what you want me to do."

She watched me with suspicious eyes as if she didn't trust me not to turn around and bail.

"Alright. There are fifteen raffle baskets, so we're going to set them up on these two tables. Each basket is numbered, and then there are the corresponding boxes that go beside them for the raffle tickets. If you want to work on one through seven, I'll put up eight through fifteen on that table."

"Sounds good."

She nodded and gave me one last suspicious look before getting to work.

The tables were already set up with blue tablecloths and white lights, pulling in the cold-as-ice theme she was going with this year. We worked together efficiently, keeping a great rhythm until someone came and called her away for another issue they needed her to deal with.

I finished up the last few baskets, then took the supplies

back to her office, where I spotted the broken sign on her desk. I hated how disappointed and almost devastated she looked when the kid told her what happened.

I found a stack of Post-It notes on her desk and left her one, letting her know I was running to the store and would be back.

While it sucked not having my truck, it was nice being in a small town where almost everything was within walking distance.

A bell dinged over my head as I walked into the hardware store, having been here a few times already since I'd been back in Sugarplum Falls. I went to the back of the store where I knew they kept the lumber and started picking the pieces I wanted. I knew that a wooden arch wouldn't be anything compared to the sign that had been broken, but the least I could do was try.

In my mind, I pictured a beautiful white arch that was wide enough to fit the bench Santa and Mrs. Claus would sit on but thin enough that Jasmin could easily store it in the supply room without it getting damaged. I grabbed a couple of 4X4s, a can of white stain, and some other necessities and headed toward the register.

I looked around for the older man who had helped me the last time I was in there but waited patiently at the register when no one appeared.

"Hi, sorry about the wait," a voice said that sent chills down my spine. My jaw clenched as I gripped the shopping cart handle harder. She came around the corner, wearing a smile on her face until she recognized me.

"Oh. Hi, son."

Twenty-Three
Brody

"Don't call me that," I snarled, refusing to lift my head to look her in the eyes.

She raised her hands in front of her, giving me space like I was a caged animal about to attack.

"Where's the older guy who works here?"

"He's out sick. It's just me today."

"Fine. I'll come back another time."

I shoved the cart off to the side, ready to slam through the door to get the hell out of there when she spoke and stopped me in my tracks.

"I'm sober, Brody. Have been for five years."

I glared at her reflection in the door as she watched me.

"I know you're angry with me, but I wanted you to know that. I don't drink anymore."

I spun around so fast that I startled myself.

"What—do you want me to say that I'm proud of you or something?" My words were like ice, seeping out of my body like the poison I felt every time I thought about her.

"No. I don't deserve that." She pulled her shoulders back

and took a deep breath. "No one has more regrets in life than me. I know that I can't change what happened in the past, and that's something I will *forever* live with. But Brody, I'm not the same person I was back then."

"You act like I care," I sneered, hating this side of me. But this anger had been living inside of me for so long that it was begging to be set free.

"I'm not asking you to care," she said softly, stepping out from behind the counter while still giving me my space. "You lost your father, and I know how hard that was for you. I lost my husband. My best friend. I was in a bad place back then, Brody. There's no way you could understand. But there was nothing, and I mean *nothing,* that I wouldn't give to change that day."

"Well, not drinking at work and passing out drunk would have been a start."

She rubbed her lips together and lowered her head.

"We can talk about all of the things I've done wrong in life, but that's not going to change anything for you, Brody. You can be as angry with me as you want. But I hope that deep down, you'll know that I have never stopped loving you. Even during my worst times, you were what brought happiness to my life. And I know I can never ask for your forgiveness, but I hope that maybe we can figure out how to live around each other now that you're back in Sugarplum Falls."

Her face was filled with hope as she said the words, but all it did was further solidify the anger that had knotted in my stomach.

"Who said I was back? I came to handle a few things and be done. My life isn't in Sugarplum Falls. It's as far away from *you* as possible."

I caught a glance at the tear that slid down her cheek before I shoved the shopping cart out of the way and left.

Twenty-Four

Jasmin

"Sorry to bother you so much," I said as I followed Hadley around to the back of Sugarplum Gifts. "I know that nothing can replace the sign, but I feel like we can't just leave that area empty. I need something Christmassy that doesn't scream *faking it until I make it*."

"I'm sorry things are so stressful right now," she replied with a soft smile. "I can only imagine the extra pressure you're feeling with the sign breaking and the whole debacle with the reindeer. Poor Mr. Truman, may he rest in peace."

"It definitely wasn't how I imagined things going this year. I plan so early, too, just to avoid having all of this stuff happen—yet it still does. I give up."

"You can't give up. You're the magic maker who brings everyone together for Frosty Fest. Without you, this town wouldn't know what to do."

"I'm sure they'd figure it out. Probably while in line for one of Sam's magical lattes or drowning their sorrows with Aiden over a glass of Dirty Reindeer Balls."

"How about this?" Hadley offered, moving a pile of stuff off to the side to show me a snow globe-style ornament with Santa and Mrs. Claus kissing inside. I tried to focus on it, but my mind was immediately distracted by the baseball glove and ball.

"Where did you get that?" I asked, pointing at it.

Her brows furrowed in confusion as she set the ornament back into its box and pulled the glove and ball over.

"Mr. Secton has been bringing stuff over as he clears out the last of everything in the pawn shop. With him closing it down, there are some collectibles, so we've been buying them from him for the store."

I held the glove in my hand and rolled it over, noticing how old it was—yet it looked brand new. Then I picked up the ball, and my heart sank.

Written in permanent marker were the words:

Merry Christmas, Brody

Love, Dad

My tears began to prickle as I realized what I was actually holding.

"How long has he had this?" I demanded, leaning forward to make sure I didn't miss her answer.

"I don't know." She shrugged, looking alarmed by my sudden interest in it. "He didn't say. I missed most of the conversation since I'm not management, but I know he said there were some personal things he was holding onto, hoping someday their rightful owner would come in to claim them. Why? What's up with the glove and ball?"

I shook my head, a surge of excitement running through me.

"Can I buy it, please?"

"I… um… I don't even know what the price is. It hasn't been entered into the system yet."

"I really need to have this. Just tell me a price or write my name down on an IOU. Whatever you need, but I really, really, really need this, Hadley."

"You're scaring me. What's with this new baseball obsession?"

"I can't explain it right now, but please." I lifted my hands in front of me and begged, blinking my eyes to make her take pity on me.

"Fine. Take it. I'll let them know to settle with you later. But if I get fired for this…." She pointed her finger at me and spun it in a circle.

"Then I'll get you a job with me, corralling the reindeer." I winked and grabbed the glove and ball from the counter, too excited to stay there for what I really needed. "Thanks, Had!"

"You owe me," she called as I flew out the door, excited to rush home and wrap it before I gave it to Brody.

150

Twenty-Five
Brody

Seeing my mom was motivational—in that it motivated me to get my ass in gear and get the hell out of town. Thankfully, the line at the automotive shop moved quickly, and the repair was easy. There was still a handful of things that needed to be fixed on the truck, but soon, they would be no longer my concern. That would stay at the ranch, with everything else, while I headed back to Wyoming.

I filled up with enough gas to get back to the ranch, then headed home without telling anyone.

I knew that Jasmin would be expecting me to come back since that was what my note said, but honestly, I was doing her a favor at this point. She deserved better than someone like me who was a mess due to someone else's negligence. But that was what addiction did to people, and I wasn't about to have Jasmin be there as I worked through the traumatic feelings that had been brought to the surface again. No one needed to be around for that.

By the time I got home, the sun was starting to set, and I knew that I needed to check the reindeer. They were the only part of all of this that I was going to miss besides Jasmin. But I just had to teach my heart that it wasn't meant to be and force myself to move on, just like I did when I lost my dad.

I was filling the last trough with food when I heard footsteps approaching. I looked up to find Jasmin bundled in a thick coat and wearing winter boots this time.

"What are you doing here?" I asked, returning my attention to the reindeer.

"I heard about what happened. People around town have been talking."

I swallowed hard, forcing down the bile that threatened to rise as she approached me, stopping to scratch the reindeer's heads along the way.

"I don't know what you're talking about."

She sighed heavily and leaned against the fence post, staring at me.

"Whatever you're here for, just let it be. I don't want to talk. I'm not interested in small-town gossip. I don't want any part of it. I'm planning to finish up the few things I need to here, then get the hell back to Wyoming." I brushed my hands on the front of my jeans and found her still staring at me, this time with tears in her eyes.

"Don't do this, Brody."

"Do what?" I threw my hands in the air and stared at her.

The reindeer moved out of the way, leaving an open space between us.

"This—Brody. This whole *I've gotta get out of here because I don't want to deal with my problems* crap."

"You don't know *shit* about my problems," I bellowed.

I expected her to flinch or back away, but instead, she stepped closer to me.

"I do know shit about your problems because you trusted me enough to confide in me. And now I'm here to help you with them and wish that you would trust me enough to allow me to be there for you."

"Be there for me for what? Huh? Nothing happened."

She tipped her head back in frustration, a slight growl escaping her throat.

"You are so incredibly stubborn and hardheaded. I know that you ran into your mom today."

"Yeah, and no one told you to come out here and try to fix something you have no idea how to."

"I'm not the one who hurt you, Brody," she said, jabbing her finger into my chest. We were only inches apart now, and I wanted nothing more than to pull her into me. To allow myself to fall apart the way I desperately wanted to.

"No, but I'm about to be the one who hurt you." I sighed heavily and took a step back. My shoulders slumped with the weight of everything, and I knew she could see through me. "You deserve better than this, Jasmin. You deserve someone who will treat you right and can take care of you the right way. Someone like Sam, who brings you coffee without you having to ask and who already knows your order."

"You really need to let that go." She scrunched her face. "Sam is amazing, and everyone loves him because he's so easy to love. But he's not a threat, Brody, and you know that. Now stop deflecting and deal with what's really bothering you."

"I'm not deflecting. You are."

"Real mature." She nodded, leaning in to rub her gloved fingers across my cheek. "Talk to me."

"I don't want to."

"I know. But you need to. Brody, you saw your mother for the first time in fifteen years. People could hear you yelling from across the street. That's how I know it didn't go well. Tell me what happened."

I wanted to push her away and insist that she leave me alone, but I also couldn't deny that her forcing her way in to be there for me meant something.

I scrubbed a hand down my face and leaned against the fence post that I knew wasn't broken.

"I didn't know she worked there. I was expecting the old man, then suddenly she was there," I started, looking at her as she stood beside me. "She said she's been clean for five years and that she's never stopped loving me, but I just couldn't see past the anger. Then she said that she hoped we could learn how to live around each other now that I was back in Sugarplum Falls, and that did it. It set me off in a way I can't even describe. After that, I wanted to get as far away from here as I could. Away from her."

"I can't even imagine how hard that was for you. I wish I had the right words to say, but I don't. I haven't experienced a loss like that before. Or had the weight of grief consume me. But Brody, it is absolutely okay to be angry as long as you work through it. You can't allow yourself to sit in it forever. That's not good for you."

"I know." I swallowed back the emotion that was rising, not wanting her to see me fall apart again. "I don't know how to move past my anger toward her. It's all that I feel when I think about what happened to my dad or how I spent five years basically raising myself after he died because she wasn't there. She was physically there but checked out long before he passed."

"Anger is an important part of the grieving process. You have to work through it, along with the sadness. If you don't, it'll never get easier. And no matter how much time passes, you're not going to get over your dad dying. That loss will forever be a part of you because he was such a big part of you."

I sniffled as a rogue tear slid down my cheek.

"I was going to wait until Christmas, but I have something for you," she said, extending her hands to take mine.

"You didn't have to get me anything."

"I know." She smiled at me over her shoulder as she led us out of the barn and out into the chilly air as we headed to her SUV.

"I was at Sugarplum Gifts today, looking for something to add above the bench where Santa and Mrs. Claus sit. While Hadley was showing me options, I found this in a pile of things they had recently taken from Mr. Secton. He owned the pawn shop in town but recently closed it so he could retire."

I looked at the brown gift bag in her hand, filled with tissue paper on top.

"I don't know much about it," she said cautiously as she

handed it to me. "But I knew I had to get it as soon as I saw it."

I held the bag in one hand and pulled the tissue paper out. My breath got stuck in my throat as I spotted the baseball glove and ball inside.

"Is this?" I asked, unable to complete the sentence. It wasn't like I had told her what the set my dad had given me looked like.

She held the bag as I pulled both out, my eyes immediately filling with tears as I read the note from my dad.

She wrapped her arms around my waist and held me as I cried, no longer able to hold it in even if I wanted to.

Twenty-Six

Jasmin

"I can't believe you were just going to leave town without saying anything," I said, nudging him in the ribs as we ate pizza on his couch. "All this work I've put in to get you to loan me the reindeer, and then you try to pull a stunt like that?"

"You've just been using me all along, haven't you?"

"Maybe." I lifted my chin and smiled smugly as his fingers tickled my sides. "But really, I would have tracked your ass down in Wyoming and stolen the reindeer from you."

"Wow. You don't joke around when it comes to Frosty Fest," he teased.

I looked up and cocked my head.

"Did you just call it Frosty Fest?"

"Oh, shit. I mean the Frozen Palooza."

I shook my head and sighed heavily, giving him the best glare I could muster.

"You're lucky you're feeding me."

"Or what, *Princess?*"

"You know what, I don't think I want to be your friend

anymore." I set my empty plate on the table and started laughing as he reached forward, tickling my sides as he pulled me down onto the couch. I sighed under the weight of his body, enjoying how it felt over mine.

"That's okay. Friends are overrated. I'd rather be lovers."

"Well, then, I guess you're gonna have to stop being a fighter and change your grumpy ways."

"You still think I'm grumpy?" He arched an eyebrow and waited for my answer.

I nodded, chewing my lip as I watched the way his hazel eyes flashed with mischief.

"I guess there's only one way to fix that." He winked and began lowering himself down my body, removing my pants and panties along the way.

"Are you sure that's not the way to fix when *I'm* grumpy?" I teased, hissing as his tongue slid in between my slit. My head rolled back as my eyes fluttered closed.

"Nope. This is the way to fix all of life's problems."

"Well then, I'm all for it."

I gripped the back of his head and held it where I wanted as he ate my pussy. He fucked me with his tongue, nearly driving me over the edge as he started sucking my clit while he slid two fingers inside.

"Yes!" I cried, already feeling the start of a mind-blowing orgasm building. "Right there!"

It wasn't like he needed the guidance. This man knew very well what he was doing and wasted no time getting me off.

I arched my back and cried out his name as I came on his face.

A few seconds later, he lifted his head, wiped his mouth, and gave me a delighted look.

"See, I'm not grumpy anymore. Problem solved."

"Hmm. I don't know. I think I'm still a little grumpy," I said coyly, waiting for him to sit down and get situated. "Maybe I should ride my frustrations out?"

"I think I like the sound of that."

I giggled as I helped him undress, not bothering to take our time since we both needed this. Once he was stripped naked, I climbed over him as he sat on the couch and started to lower myself.

"Oh, wait. Did you want to use a condom this time?" I asked, pulling my shirt over my head and tossing it to the pile of clothes on the floor.

"Nope. You feel too good without one, and we're both good. Now ride your frustrations out, Princess."

I smiled as I slowly moved myself down over his cock, loving that he was already hard for me. It was different this time, but that connection I had felt the first time was still there. Heck, maybe even stronger now.

Once he was fully seated inside me, I leaned forward, allowing him access as he greedily fondled my breasts. He pulled one nipple into his mouth, sucking hard while guiding my hips with his hands on my hips. I loved how full it felt having him inside me and couldn't imagine ever going back to anything other than this again.

I reached down to rub my clit while he sucked the other nipple, both of us already close to coming. I bounced harder, rotating my hips as I ground against him. His grip on my hips deepened, holding me in place as he lifted his hips and thrust up into me.

It was like he was some sort of sex god, knowing exactly what my body needed and when. I rubbed harder, and within seconds, I came on his cock while he released his load inside of me.

Twenty-Seven

Brody

Jasmin wasn't kidding when she said that everyone showed up for Frosty Fest. We'd been at the mall since five this morning, getting everything set up, and every time I passed by the front entrance, the number of people setting up for the parade grew larger. They didn't seem to care that it was freezing outside or that the parade didn't start for another hour. They showed up for something they loved, and that warmed my heart in a way I never would have imagined.

"Hey, do you have a minute?" I asked Jasmin as she headed for her office.

"Yeah. Sure. What's up?"

She had been going a mile a minute, and even with all of the help we had, it seemed like there was still a ton to get done.

"I have something for you."

Her brows rose slightly as a smile graced her lips.

"You didn't have to get me anything."

"I didn't technically *get* it. I made it."

I felt my cheeks burn as they flushed with color. I had never made anything for anyone before, and I had no idea if she was going to hate it. When I first started, it seemed like the perfect idea. But now that I had to show it to her, I was reconsidering everything.

"Brody!" she exclaimed, covering her mouth with her hands. She hadn't even seen it yet and she was already touched by the gesture. This did nothing to calm the nerves that were making me slightly nauseous.

"It's okay if you hate it," I started, leading her to the storage room where I hid it this morning with the help of Sam and Aiden.

"Why would I hate it?" She pulled her brows together and narrowed her eyes.

I shrugged, unsure of what to say.

"I don't know. People don't like things sometimes. It's okay if you don't. My feelings won't be hurt."

"I'm sure I'm going to love whatever it is if you'll ever get around to actually *showing* me," she teased with a wink.

I pulled in a deep breath and forced it out through my mouth as I tugged the white sheet and pulled it off. She gasped as her eyes widened and she quickly made her way over to the arch.

She ran her fingers along the distressed wood frame and then touched the sign hanging from the middle. It wasn't the same as the light-up sign that had been broken, but I felt it was a nice replacement. I'd used a spare piece of wood that I had left over and stained it red before hand painting *Santa & Mrs. Claus* in a shimmery silver.

"Brody, this is amazing," she whispered. "I can't believe

you did this. When did you even have the time to do this?"

I shoved my hands in my pockets to keep from fidgeting and rocked back on my heels.

"I had some free time to kill this past week while my *girlfriend* was busy getting things set up for the Frozen Palooza," I joked, grinning like a fool.

I'd spent a lot of that time going through stuff at the ranch now that I had decided to stay. In addition to the tools I found in the shop to make the arch, I also found a handful of journals that my grandfather had kept. They seemed to start shortly after I left, but they always had an entry after we'd talk on the phone, with him mentioning how proud he was of me. It was nice to have another piece of him to hold onto now that he was gone.

"I can't believe you thought I wouldn't like it. Brody, words can't even begin to describe what this means to me. It's gorgeous, but the fact that you took the time to do something like this for me… It just… I…"

She shook her head, frustrated she couldn't get the words out as tears dotted the corners of her eyes. I stepped in front of her and pulled her against my chest as I kissed the top of her head.

"I love you too, Jasmin," I said, surprised by how easy it was to admit that.

Her head whipped up as she looked at me, likely questioning whether I meant to say it.

"I do. I love you, you crazy boot lady."

She laughed and playfully shoved my chest.

"And I love you, you grumpy ass."

I lowered my head as our lips grazed each other's.

"You guys just said you loved each other for the first time, didn't you?" Sam's voice broke through, ending the kiss.

I looked up to find him standing in the doorway with Aiden by his side as they both grinned at us.

"You would be falling in love with him too if he made you something like this," Jasmin said, wiping her eyes with one hand while keeping an arm wrapped around my waist.

"I'm more of a sandwich kind of guy," Aiden replied with a shrug. "If someone makes me a mean sandwich, I'm a goner."

Jasmin quickly turned her head and hid against my chest as laughter erupted from her.

"What's that about?" Sam questioned with a grin as he pointed at her.

"Nothing," I lied. "She's just remembering the first sandwich I made for her. That was when she realized just how much she enjoyed mayonnaise."

Twenty-Eight

Jasmin

"Alright, you guys. It's almost show time," I said loudly, grabbing everyone's attention in the mall. Aside from the vendors who were finishing setting up, it was all volunteers and those who were going to be in the parade that started in less than twenty minutes.

"I want to go over a few things before we get started. First, safety is our number one priority. While we're all here to have fun, I need all of the elves on their best behavior today. That means *no* jumping off of the floats and no mooning the crowd. I'm talking to you two," I said, pointing a finger at the rowdy Mayer twins. They were eight and kept me on my toes.

"The parade will be the same as every year. The reindeer will start, and the Sugarplum Falls High School marching band will follow. After that, the floats are already lined up and ready to go. Each float will have a handful of elves that will be responsible for tossing candy canes into the crowd. Try to make sure you guys are spacing it out so we don't run out in the first five minutes like we did a few years ago. Adult elves, it'll be your responsibility to monitor your supply and to make sure you have enough to get through the entire parade."

They all nodded and continued to give me their undivided

attention as one of our littlest elves made a run for it.

"We have an elf on the loose," I announced, pointing in the direction of the toddler who was running with a handful of candy canes they had stolen.

"After the parade is over, we'll all meet back in the break room. There will be hot chocolate and plenty of food. I'll ask that everyone take a look at the list taped to the door so they know who is supposed to take their break and when. It's important that we're ready to go as soon as the parade is over. We'll need Santa and Mrs. Claus to get ready while the elves start lining the kids up for pictures."

I smiled as one of the adult elves wrangled the runaway toddler and kept them entertained while I finished the speech everyone probably already had memorized.

"Today is going to be an amazing day, and from the bottom of my heart, thank you all for being here and helping out. Without you guys, Frosty Fest wouldn't be what it is. It warms my heart every year when I see how many people volunteer to do this. You guys are the real MVPs."

"I thought that was the reindeer," one of the teenage boys said, a smirk crossing his face.

"Well, they are also very important to our event. But I wouldn't be able to do any of this without the help of the town. From volunteers to the vendors, everyone contributes. That's an amazing thing, and it just goes to show how incredible Sugarplum Falls is. Now, everyone, help yourself to a sugar cookie and get ready. The parade starts in ten minutes."

They all cheered and then began heading off to where they

needed to go. Thankfully, many of the volunteers were experienced, so they were able to help guide those who were new and unsure of what to do.

I finished what I needed to do, then made my way outside to help make sure everything and everyone was in place.

People were already lining the street, sitting on the sidewalk as they waited for the parade to start. The crowd was bigger this year than I'd ever seen, which left me both nervous and excited about how busy the mall would be with the extra traffic. But there was nothing that could be done about that now. Hopefully, multiple vendors would end up selling out today and have a great day for sales.

As I walked past everyone, I felt eyes on me and looked up to find Brody watching me. He was standing near the front, by where the reindeer were, and it pulled at my heart that Mr. Truman wasn't there. It was strange not seeing him there and brought a sadness over me at the loss we were all suffering without him.

"Thank you for bringing the reindeer," I said, my throat tight with emotion. "It means a lot to me," I paused and looked around, "to all of us."

He nodded, his eyes getting glossy as well.

"My pleasure."

He reached for my hand and gave it a quick squeeze as I struggled to keep the tears in.

"You were right," he said, bringing my attention back to him. "This is an amazing turnout. I can see why it means so much to you. To the town. I've never seen anything like it before. I'm sorry I was such a pain about it."

"Well, get ready to see some Christmas magic," I whispered, kissing his cheek before rushing off as they waited for me to get the parade started.

Twenty- Nine

Brody

She wasn't lying. That parade felt magical. It wasn't just the children singing Christmas songs at the top of their lungs that made it feel special. It was the way everyone was smiling and seemed genuinely happy like they *wanted* to be there.

After it was over, I got the reindeer settled in the pen outside that Jasmin had set up for the kids to come see them and then went inside the mall to find Jasmin. I knew she would be working the rest of the day, but I wanted to help however I could. Even if that meant I had to put on one of the ridiculous elf costumes and guide the sugar-crazed kids in line to see Santa.

I headed into the breakroom where she told me she would be and was surprised by how many people were already in there. There were so many little elves running around that I was convinced we had to be at the North Pole.

"Alright, little elves, you're done for the day. Grab some lunch and your parents will be in to get you shortly. Junior elves, you have about fifteen minutes before you need to head out to your assigned station. Most of the vendors are fine, but work your way through the different booths to see if they need anything. Those working at the Santa station have an hour before you start. Have lunch and take a break.

Catie will be in here for the rest of the day so go to her with any questions if you can't find me."

There were a bunch of mumbled responses as I made my way around the children and caught up with Jasmin.

"Hey," she said, leaning in to hug me. "What did you think of the parade?"

"Pure magic."

"I knew I could make you love Christmas," she teased, kissing me softly on the lips.

"You didn't make me love Christmas, Princess. You made me love you."

"So you still don't love Christmas?"

I shrugged, not wanting to disappoint her.

"It hasn't even happened yet, so there's still time."

She pouted, but I could tell it was just an act.

"Where are you headed now?" I asked, lacing my fingers in hers as we walked out of the breakroom and into the mall.

"The giving tree. Santa and Mrs. Claus are heading there shortly."

"Mind if I join you?"

"Not at all. This is my favorite part, so I would love for you to be here to experience it, too."

"I thought the reindeer were your favorite part?" I teased, lowering my brows at her. "Were you just saying that to get me to give them to you?"

Her jaw dropped open as a blush crossed her face.

"No! I love them too! This is just different. I love both, but not the same."

"I'm just giving you a hard time."

"Well, maybe you can give me a *real hard time* later," she whispered, trying not to move her mouth as we approached the crowd that was already waiting.

"I'm going to say hi to a few people, then I need to go up and give a quick speech. After that, I'll come join you. Okay?"

I nodded and smiled as she rushed off.

I stood to the side, making sure we had a good spot to watch everything without being in the way. I felt someone tug on my arm and moved to the side to get out of their way.

"Brody Truman," an old, gruff voice said, startling me.

I looked beside me to see an older man with silver hair and a checkered cardigan wrapped around his frail body.

"Hi," I replied, a little uncertainty in my voice. "Do I know you?"

He shook his head and stood beside me. His eyes stayed locked on the tree in front of us as he rested his hands on the cane he was using to walk.

"I've been waiting to see you," he commented, still not looking at me. "At my age, tracking people down gets to be too much work. But I trusted that I would run into you when the time was right."

"Okay…" I didn't want to be rude, but I had no idea who he was or what he was talking about.

"Eighteen years ago, a distraught woman walked into my pawn shop," he started, and my heart sank. I lowered my head, not sure that I was ready to hear the story. "She was crying, telling me how she needed to sell something to be able to put food on the table because her husband had died."

My jaw tightened as I continued to listen.

"I already knew who she was, just like I knew she wasn't using the money I gave her to buy food. Her dad, your grandpa, and I were best friends. I knew all about Tabitha's drinking problem and that she was going to use the money to feed her addiction."

I looked at him, tears forming in my eyes no matter how hard I tried to hold them back.

"Then why did you give her the money?" I asked. "If you knew she was just going to use it to buy more alcohol, why did you enable her?"

"I didn't." He turned and looked at me, sadness washing over his face. "I talked to your grandpa, and his heart sank when I told him what I'd done. I wasn't proud of it, Son. But I've waited eighteen years to tell you why I did it."

"Okay," I said with a shaky breath. "Why did you do it?"

"Because I was given an opportunity to save a piece of your dad for you. I never had any intention of selling that baseball glove and ball. It never even went into the store. I gave her the money for it so I could make sure it stayed safe until I could give it to you. I knew that if I didn't give her the money for it, she would find someone who would. I couldn't stand the thought of that. To have the last gift your dad gave you get thrown away like it meant nothing broke my heart the way it did yours. So, I gave her the money, and I've been holding onto it ever since."

"Why didn't my grandfather ever tell me?"

He shrugged and looked down at his cane.

"I think he was torn on what to do. He knew that it would be hard for you to come back and see your mother. He didn't want you to come back until you were ready to, and as the years passed, it seemed like that would never be the case. We both forgot about it after some time. It wasn't until I started cleaning stuff out after I closed the pawn shop that I found it. I didn't know you were back in town, and the thought of handing it over to the gift shop instead of finding you nearly killed me. But my health isn't the best, Son. I didn't have much choice."

I nodded, my throat too tight to speak.

"Hadley told me about Jasmin taking it, so I came here today to talk to her about who the rightful owner is. But then I saw you two together and realized that fate had already worked everything out. I'm glad it's back where it belongs."

"Thank you," I whispered, still overwhelmed with emotion.

He smiled and gave me a nod before walking off, carefully moving his cane through the crowd to keep from falling.

Thirty

Jasmin

Christmas Day

I woke up to the snow falling and Brody's arm wrapped tightly around my waist.

"Good morning," he said sleepily, pulling me against his chest as he kissed the spot on the back of my neck that drove me crazy.

"Good morning. Merry Christmas." I was nervous about saying it because even though a lot had changed in only a few weeks, I had no idea how he felt about the holiday. Between seeing his mom for the first time since he left and getting the gift back that his dad had given to him, it had been a roller coaster of emotions.

"Merry Christmas."

I rolled onto my back and looked up at him. It was nice having him in bed beside me and I was getting way too used to constantly sharing a bed with him. We hadn't talked much about what our future looked like since he technically lived out at the ranch. It wasn't like he was going to up and sell it to move in with me—especially since I didn't have anywhere to keep the reindeer. And he hadn't asked me to move in with him, so we just took turns staying at each other's places and keeping a handful of our stuff at both.

"So, how do you spend Christmas morning?" he asked.

"Well, I usually get up and fix myself a cup of coffee and something to eat since Sugarplum Lattes has the audacity to be closed today. Then I FaceTime my parents and we open presents together. I don't have any family in town, so I kinda just hang out. Read a book or watch a movie. Then, every year, I go to Sugar Faced Bar for dinner. A small group of us get together and do a potluck, but it's nice to have company."

"Sounds like fun. Should I start by making us some breakfast?"

"Are you going to make it porn-style like you did the sandwiches?" I teased, still unable to get that image out of my head.

"I don't know. Are you craving something with mayonnaise?" He wiggled his eyebrows and then gently rolled me over and spanked my ass. "Or maybe it's just the spanking you're into."

I nodded and allowed him to rub the spot he'd turned red before spanking me again. It was something both of us were into, and I had no problem delaying the phone call with my parents if that meant we had a little time for fun this morning.

"Nope. Get out of bed," he said, shaking his head as if reading my thoughts. "I'll start breakfast. You start the coffee. We'll eat, and then I have a few gifts I'd like you to open."

I rolled over and climbed off the bed, wrapping the robe he handed me around my naked body.

"You didn't have to get me anything. I told you that."

He pulled his joggers over his hips and cocked his head to stare at me.

"What?" I laughed nervously. "I'm serious. You didn't have to."

"What kind of asshole do you think I am that I wouldn't buy my girlfriend a present for Christmas?"

I shrugged and scrunched my face.

"The kind that hates Christmas?" I offered.

"*Used* to hate Christmas," he corrected as we walked to the kitchen. "I can move past that and give the holiday another chance, you know?"

"So are you saying that you *love* Christmas now?" I grabbed the bag of coffee and started making a pot.

"No. But I'm saying that I *love* you."

"I love you too." I leaned up and kissed him as we passed each other. We'd gotten so used to moving around each other in the kitchen that this was just natural for us now. He got started on breakfast while I pulled the dishes down and put Christmas music on the TV.

We ate quickly and then called my parents, who were just delighted to meet Brody. By the end of the call, they had already made plans to come down and visit so they could meet my new boyfriend in person. It made my heart happy to see how happy they were.

Once we were done, we took some time to relax and open each other's gifts. I had purposely restrained myself from getting him a ton of stuff because I didn't want to overwhelm him. I still had no idea how to spend the holiday with a boyfriend, so I didn't want to scare him off right out of the gate.

"Open mine first," he said, handing me a small box wrapped in white shimmery paper with a blue ribbon around it. I smiled, realizing that it would go perfectly with the cold-as-ice theme we did for Frosty Fest.

"I love the wrapping," I commented, gently untying the ribbon.

"Well, I know how much you love the Frozen Palooza, so I stuck with the theme."

"Frosty Fest." I raised my eyebrows in warning. "And I only went with the theme because you wouldn't stop calling it the Frozen Palooza. It seemed fitting that it should be cold as ice."

He grinned and leaned back against the couch as I opened the lid to the box and pulled out a delicate necklace. There was a silver charm with the word *princess* in the center of the thin silver chain.

"You know, this name has started to grow on me," I said with a smile. "This is beautiful. Thank you, Brody."

"You're welcome. It was a bitch to get the name right, but after a few hundred attempts, I finally had one I liked. Hand cutting metal is not for the impatient."

"You made this?" My eyebrows rose nearly as high as my voice.

He nodded.

"Wow. You really can do everything, can't you?"

"I wouldn't say everything."

"Brody, this is seriously amazing. I've seen some of the stuff you've welded, but then you add on your woodworking expertise and now this? You seriously need a booth at Frosty Fest next year."

He let his head fall back as he laughed, the sound something I never thought I'd hear out of him.

"I'm glad you like it."

"Like it? No. I don't like it. I love it. Seriously." I lifted the necklace to my neck and gently secured it, worried I might accidentally break something. "Okay, now you open my gift."

I handed him a box that was heavier than it looked. He ripped the paper off and grinned when he saw the outside cover of what was inside.

"I know how much you enjoy making sandwiches," I said with a simple shrug as he held up the panini press. "Now you can make fancy ones."

"You just want me to finger the mayo again."

"Maybe." I licked my lips and laughed along with him.

"Well, we can talk about that later. But I have another gift I want you to open now." He handed me a small box that almost resembled a ring box, and my heart fluttered. "Just open it," he pushed with a crooked smile, reading my mind again.

I slowly pushed the lid open and stared at a silver key inside.

"It's to the ranch," he said, clearing his throat. "I know that you have your life out here and that it might be a bit presumptuous of me to ask, but would you move in with me?"

I blinked rapidly, trying to force the tears away as emotion rushed through me.

"You want me to live with you?" I held up the key, not sure that this was real. It felt too good to be true.

"I do. And to be honest, so do the reindeer. I've seen how much they love you, Jasmin. Almost as much as I do."

I wiped away my tears as I nodded yes. He reached over the pile of wrapping paper sitting on the floor between us and pulled me over to him.

"I need to hear it."

"Yes, Brody. I'll move in with the reindeer," I teased playfully, giggling when he tickled my sides. "Okay, okay! I'll move in with you *and* the reindeer."

"That's more like it." He nipped the bottom of my ear before planting a kiss on my cheek.

We opened the rest of the presents and then got ready for dinner. It felt weird taking someone since I always went solo, but at the same time, I was giddy with excitement. Brody had really come out of his shell and gotten to know everyone better—even Sam. And just like I expected, everyone loved him.

"Are you sure they're here?" he asked, leaning forward to look out the windshield as the snow fell heavily in front of us.

"Yeah, we all park in the back so out-of-towners don't think it's open. If you pull around there, you'll see everyone's cars." I pointed to where I wanted him to go.

We got out, and Brody carried the crockpot full of turkey inside while I grabbed the gift bags. It was always a small gathering, but for some of us, this was the only Christmas celebration we had so we did a gift exchange. It was Aiden's idea after he realized how many people used to come into the bar on Christmas because they had nowhere else to go, and he had no one to spend the holiday with.

I pulled open the door and held it with my hip so Brody could go in first. Sam and Aiden were already there, setting up the rest of the food on the table they set out for tonight. I put my gifts on the other table with the few that were already there and then went to see what I could help with.

"Merry Christmas," I said, pulling Aiden in for a hug. "Thanks for hosting again."

"Merry Christmas. Always my pleasure."

Brody said hello to Aiden while I hugged Sam.

Soon, everyone started piling in and we gathered around the table to enjoy dinner as a family. My heart felt full and happy as I spent Christmas with the people I loved.

****

Want to hang out and chat books? Find me in my reader group on Facebook

https://www.facebook.com/groups/2945710968775398/

Ready for more steamy holiday romance? Be sure to check out the rest of the Sugarplum Falls series or dive into one of my standalone holiday books!

Blame It On The Mistletoe
https://books2read.com/u/bw1rqe

Blame It On The Eggnog
https://books2read.com/u/38PPY6

Blame It On The Candy Canes
https://books2read.com/u/31DNo7

Blame It On The Blizzard
https://books2read.com/u/b6z6XE

Snow Place To Go

https://books2read.com/u/4A560N

A Very Merry Kissmas

https://books2read.com/u/bPDgy7

A Christmas Wish

https://books2read.com/u/4EKXpE

Holiday Hijinks

https://books2read.com/u/4DP6Ze

Other Books By Samantha Baca

The Haven Brook Series
(small-town romantic suspense):

'Til Death Do Us Part (Haven Brook Book 1)

https://books2read.com/u/m2RJNR

The Cradle Will Fall (Haven Brook Book 2)

https://books2read.com/u/b6O0QE

The Ties That Bind (Haven Brook Book 3)

https://books2read.com/u/mqgoz8

A Very Haven Christmas (Haven Brook Book 4- Novella)

https://books2read.com/u/mvqGjj

Three Strikes, You're Gone (Haven Brook Book 5)

https://books2read.com/u/mvqL2z

<u>The Dark Shadows Trilogy</u>
<u>(romantic suspense)</u>

Five Steps Ahead (Dark Shadows Book 1)

https://books2read.com/u/38Q0gO

Ten Seconds Too Late (Dark Shadows Book 2)

https://books2read.com/u/3JRgVB

Against The Clock (Dark Shadows Book 3)

https://books2read.com/u/m2YwoR

<u>The Stone Creek Series</u>
<u>(small-town- novellas)</u>

Chocolate Covered Mistletoe (Stone Creek Book 1)

https://books2read.com/u/3LRk9N

Candy Coated Promises (Stone Creek Book 2)

https://books2read.com/u/mldP5Y

Pumpkin Spiced Possibilities (Stone Creek Book 3)

https://books2read.com/u/bojdwV

<u>Beaumont Creek Series</u>
<u>(small town)</u>

Just One Time (Beaumont Creek Book 1)

https://books2read.com/u/3G52zK

Second Chances (Beaumont Creek Book 2)

https://books2read.com/u/4Aj6Z0

Third Time's The Charm (Beaumont Creek Book 3)

https://books2read.com/u/b5lEyG

Four-ever Single (Beaumont Creek Book 4)

https://books2read.com/u/4j5jMX

Fifth Wheel (Beaumont Creek Book 5)

https://books2read.com/u/4XwKwa

<u>Whiskey Mountain Series (small-town- novellas)</u>

Something To Talk About

https://books2read.com/u/4X62ag

Something To Think About

https://books2read.com/u/3GWAan

Something To Believe In

https://books2read.com/u/3yVzgB

Something To Live For

https://books2read.com/u/mllEOP

<u>Sugarplum Falls Series (Holiday Novellas- can be read as standalone)</u>

Blame It On The Mistletoe
https://books2read.com/u/bw1rqe

Blame It On The Eggnog
https://books2read.com/u/38PPY6

Blame It On The Candy Canes
https://books2read.com/u/31DNo7

Blame It On The Blizzard
https://books2read.com/u/b6z6XE

Blame It On The Reindeer
https://books2read.com/u/baLAG6

Blame It On The Carols
https://books2read.com/u/me8E9z

Blame It On The Lattes
https://books2read.com/u/mB1E2A

Blame It On The Secret Santa
https://books2read.com/u/mY9dGY

<u>Standalone Books</u>

One Last Wish

https://books2read.com/u/mqg7D9

Finding Love In Apartment 2C (novella)

https://books2read.com/u/bze9aZ

Cocky Counsel: A Hero Club Novel

https://books2read.com/u/31Kzkn

All Is Fair In Food And War (novella)

https://books2read.com/u/bp8qjX

Holiday Books
(novellas)

Snow Place To Go

https://books2read.com/u/4A560N

A Very Merry Kissmas

https://books2read.com/u/bPDgy7

A Christmas Wish

https://books2read.com/u/4EKXpE

Holiday Hijinks

https://books2read.com/u/4DP6Ze

Acknowledgments

Thank you for reading this book and for supporting my dreams of being an author. I know that probably seems like such a simple thing to say, but I mean it from the bottom of my heart. Without readers, authors wouldn't have a reason to write. So, thank you.

As always, I want to extend a huge thank you to my alpha and beta readers for all of their help in making this book as amazing as possible. Amanda, Azucena, Claire, and Valerie, thank you, ladies, for taking so much time going through this book and helping me through the first go-round. And the second. And third… But seriously, each of you brings so much value, and your feedback is always appreciated.

Malissa and Jackie, you both are always so fabulous and helpful with finding stuff we've missed the first few hundred times. I can't begin to think about what a sad day it would be not to have you both on my team helping me. Thank you for everything you do!

Tamara, thank you for jumping in as a beta reader and helping with the story! I appreciate you and your love for my books!

My ARC readers are some of the absolute best there are, and I love and appreciate every single one of you. Thank you for taking a chance on my book. I hope it provided some happiness and a little comedic relief if needed.

To my family—I write the same thing with every book because no matter what changes in life, I will never stop thanking you for your love and support. I love you guys!

We all know that my husband is the biggest dick in the

world, and that's why I love him. If you're not sure why I say that, be sure to come hang out in my reader group. Richard, you haven't divorced me yet—even after 32 books! I have hope we can keep doing this book thing and get to the point where you retire from your regular job and come work for me. Big dreams, I know. But we're getting one step closer every day. I love you. Thanks for being awesome.

My sweet girls who are getting so big… You still know how to make me smile with your unwavering support for my writing. I don't know what I would do without you. But I hope that no matter what life brings, you always chase your dreams. Never settle for mediocre because you were both made for amazing things. I love you both so much!

About the Author

Samantha lives in the southwest with her husband and two small children after abandoning her childhood dream of living in a cabin in Colorado when she found that she couldn't afford to live there and was deathly allergic to the woods. When she's not writing, she's usually spouting off sarcastic remarks while drinking wine out of a coffee mug to look like a functional adult while chasing down her toddlers. She enjoys spending time with her family, watching reruns of Friends, and the 24/7 flow of coffee that can be found in her veins. Be sure to follow her on social media for updates on what she's working on.

You can find her here:

Facebook: https://www.facebook.com/AuthorSamanthaBaca

Instagram: https://instagram.com/author_samantha_baca

Goodreads: http://www.goodreads.com/authorsamanthabaca

Facebook Reader Group:https://www.facebook.com/groups/2945710968775398/

Webpage: https://authorsamanthabaca.wordpress.com

Newsletter: http://eepurl.com/g0NcSj

www.ingramcontent.com/pod-product-compliance
Lightning Source LLC
Chambersburg PA
CBHW031046310726
48969CB00007B/2137